A JOURNEY THROUGH LOVE, PAIN AND HEALING

THE SMILE THAT SPOKE AT LAST

A BOOK BY

KALYANI LONKAR

BlueRose ONE
Stories Matter
NewDelhi • London

BLUEROSE PUBLISHERS
India | U.K.

For permissions requests or inquiries regarding this publication, please contact:

BLUEROSE PUBLISHERS
www.BlueRoseONE.com
info@bluerosepublishers.com
+91 8882 898 898
+4407342408967

ISBN: 978-93-6783-483-1

Cover design: Shubham
Typesetting: Sagar

First Edition: January 2025

Travelling in Pandemic

Locked in her hotel room for the past 7 days, Ira found herself pondering over the unexpected turn her life had taken. The monotony of the room heightened her reflection on the recent events that led her to this point. With her persistent headache and her phone silenced, she decided to elevate her stress by brewing a good cup of coffee. Seated by the window, and Ira grazed the plants, the garden and the pool in between, her mind was unusually quiet, which was filled with things that would never allow her to rest.

Her long journey from London to Mumbai had taken a week ago, which felt like just yesterday she was alone at the airport with the bags and thinking about how she was going to get through the mess that was complicated and hard for anyone to understand. Another thing was the chaos of travelling in the pandemic which she read on some Facebook on how to do it and what not to do. She recalled the early morning on February 12th 2021, waking up at 2am, ready for her flight back to India. A hasty interaction with her husband, Kartik, reflected the detachment that had grown in between them. The first and last hug before leaving, devoid of emotion, marked the end of 13 months and 20 days spent in a relationship that had lost its meaning.

At Woodside Park in London, an hour-long ride in a cab to the airport made Ira stoic, her mind racing with the months that she considered wasted. The peculiar mix of feelings intensified when she reminisced about the wired-looking cow bear teddy that her so called husband had given to her a day before. No wonder Ira hated the gift and never even found it as cute as Kartik thought it was. At Heathrow Airport, 5 hours before the flight, she calculated the expenses that had been incurred during her journey, including Covid-19 tests, as she had to take them multiple times as the flights were getting cancelled multiple times. Each test costed her like £120, and she had to take those 7 times which was

£840, apart from the sacrifices that she had made for this transformative journey.

In the midst of her journey, Ira reflected on the sacrifices that she had made for a crumbling marriage. It wasn't Kartik's footing bills; she was the one financing her escape. The patience, the courage that she had shown surprised even her closest of friends, who had never seen her endure such an insult, as Ira was known to be a strong-headed person who would kill people with her strong words if anyone would disrespect her. But here she was insulted on an everyday basis, and the word respect was not present in Kartik's dictionary. Living in a self–created illusion that she could fix everything, Ira finally shattered the bubble in November 2020 when she wasn't able to endure any more pain, and for whom? This idiot? Opening up to her elder sister Meera, she exposed the pain, loneliness and the unravelling marriage.

At the airport, Ira struggled with her baggage, physically burdened by the weight of her emotions. Heading to the Air India check–in counter, she expressed gratitude for the "Vande Bharat Program," allowing the Indians to return home. She thanked her friend Ravi Chandra, who played a crucial role in keeping her informed and providing necessary documentation. Despite Ravi being someone she once envisioned as her life partner but guess what destiny had other plans. Swiftly completing immigration, Ira prepared for the flight to India.

On the Air India flight, filled with exuberant Marwari and Gujarati passengers, she yearned for a moment of peace. Hoping leaving early or boarding the flight would heal her broken heart, she found solace only in her imagination. Hungry and tired, she braved the journey, confronting memories with every passing moment. Nine hours later, upon landing in Mumbai, the only thought occupying her mind was the prospect of collapsing into a bed and embracing the much-needed sleep.

Entering the next phase of her journey, Ira anticipated the upcoming challenges with a newfound confidence and covered all her bases by filling out all necessary forms – an assumption that soon would be dispelled. Upon landing at Chhatrapati Shivaji Maharaj International Airport in Mumbai, Ira joined the line for self-reporting form for international travelers, the process surprisingly took only five minutes. The next challenge awaited in the Arogya Setu form line, which she had failed to fill in, which took quite a lot of time. Later, standing in the crowd of confused travellers, Ira completed the form, realizing the mandatory 7-day institutional quarantine for international arrivals in Maharashtra.

As she spoke with fellow travelers, she gathered information and insights. When her turn arrived, she presented the form to an airport official, who guided her to a list of hotels for quarantine. Drawing on her pre–research from platforms like YouTube and the "Indians in London" Facebook page, Ira had specific criteria in mind while choosing a hotel:

1. A room with a window for natural light and a view of the outside world.
2. A clean, spacious room allowing for activities like walking, dancing or exercise.
3. Good food options, including both vegetarian and non-vegetarian, with the possibility of room service.
4. A place with a bar menu to provide moments of distraction.
5. A reasonable cost, preferably within the range of 3000–4000 Rs per day to align with her budget.

Navigating the challenges of quarantine with foresight and a touch of humor, Ira prepared for the next leg of the journey which she never thought would turn into Mumbai darshan. (short trip in Mumbai)

In the new phase of her journey, Ira armed with research, opted for the Kohinoor Continental hotel after the Lemon Tree was fully booked. She secured a room with meals for Rs 3000 and promptly informed the officials. Directed to the basement, she joined the queue at 1:20 am on February 13th, realizing an hour had passed since her landing. Navigating through various counters, she shared her travelling details. Boarding a bus with a limited capacity of 5 passengers, she encountered fellow travellers conversing in Hindi, Marathi and English, feeling the unmistakable shift of being in India.

The journey to find hotel of each passenger was like having a late-night stroll in the quiet streets of Mumbai; the usual streets were surprisingly quite almost surreal, at 2:30am. Engaging in conversation with Ira, a vet surgeon from London, Ira learned more about veganism and the fascinating process drop at Taj Hotel due to quarantine rules. Though tempted, Taj was full of travelers. While travelling, Ira shared stories about their favorite foods, clubs and place to visit. Natasha, a vegan and Ira discussed the importance of health and were both amused by a fellow passenger choosing a seemingly haunted hotel for quarantine.

After several drop–offs they reached Kohinoor Elite, which was not the correct hotel. A brief argument ensues, but Ira shows her original form, stating that Kohinoor Continental. Upon arrival, she signed the papers, paid Rs 28,000 for 7 days and received a stern set of rules from the airport officials. Confined to Room 309 in A wing, she texted her husband, father, younger brother Ishan, elder sister Meera and friend Ravi of her safe arrival to the room. Switching off her phone, she ordered a sandwich, for which she had to convince them as to how she has not had any food for the past 10 hours and might die. Hence, they should feed her, and they did. Ira thought the headache will subside with some food but when it didn't help as much, she took a pain killer and eventually succumbed to a deep sleep, having been awake for more than 48hrs.

Institutional Quarantine

Day 1: February 13th, 2021

Ira's first day in quarantine began with a struggle to wake up at 4 pm, her sleep disrupted by breakfast and lunch deliveries. She was too exhausted to care, even hanging a face mask on the door for convenience. After a couple of hours, she reluctantly turned on her phone, finding a text from her estranged husband, Kartik, giving her "permission" to sleep. Her father had called and messaged, offering financial support and expressing happiness at her return. Ravi advised her to rest, while her younger brother, Ishan, and elder sister, Meera, welcomed her to India. Meera's barrage of questions irked Ira, especially when probed about Kartik.

In a contemplative moment, Ira opened the curtains to a blurred window overlooking Andheri Metro station, missing the clear view she once had. Dinner arrived at 8:30 pm, with a friendly waiter making a comment about her seemingly constant presence at the door. The meal consisted of paneer curry, potato curry, pickle, rice, dal, salad, four small rotis, and a tiny piece of cake. Ira found the curry spicy, enjoyed the dal and rice, but felt the dessert was insufficient. Tired but not enough for a shower, she settled on her bed, opened her laptop, and explored Netflix. A message to Ravi led to an hour-long phone call, providing a sense of comfort amid the challenges of the day.

It's hard to let go when emotions run high,
No matter the choice, we can't just pass by.
That last hug felt like counting the days,
As night turns to day, the moments vanished away.

Day 2: 14th February 2021 - Valentine's Day

Valentine's Day in quarantine was a unique celebration for Ira. Eager to embrace her newfound freedom, she had purchased an expensive bottle of red wine at the Mumbai airport. Encouraged by friends to enjoy her independence, she decided to have a grand celebration in her hotel room. She danced energetically to loud music from the 90s, dressed up as if expecting friends to join her for a drink.

Excitement turned to solitude as the reality of being alone hit her; despite ordering pizza, her favourite dessert Gulab jamun, and fancy wine glass from room service, she couldn't escape the fact that she was stuck in a challenging situation. Staring at the glass of wine, she pondered her journey, knowing she would face criticism upon returning home, having never disclosed her failing marriage to her parents.

Despite the emotional turmoil, Ira, an assertive individual, acknowledged that nothing could hold her back now. Determined to overcome the challenges ahead, she found solace in the thought that with her education, she could navigate the difficult path ahead. It was 3 am when she realized she should eat and watch a comforting show before attempting to sleep. Suffering from jetlag, she felt tired but not sleepy. Planning to take a shower, the warm water triggered tears, not of guilt, but a release of emotions accumulated during her challenging journey. She wept, hoping for closure and an end to her struggles.

After all the tears had been shed, she found herself pondering the question: What is marriage, seriously? Reflecting on all the experiences she had been through, she couldn't help but question the true essence of marriage.

What is Marriage?

Marriage, often discussed as a lifelong commitment, seems surrounded by a lot of hype. Ira, 28, still single and residing in Pune. In India, the societal pressure for a girl to marry intensifies after crossing 25, as if time is running out. Personally, I find this notion absurd. While everyone around me is settling down, being single has its own allure.

Ira used to have a vibrant group of friends from her society, including Shruti(B), Rutuja, Ankita (Anki), Rupali (Mau), Monica (Monu), Tanmayee, Gauri, Arundhati, Ekta, Amruta, and her. They shared great times from college to late-night badminton matches. Eventually, one by one, they all got married. Among them, Rupali (Mau) was Ira's closest companion, and even today, they share everything. Sometimes, they jokingly think if she were a guy, Ira might have married her.

Unlike her friend Mau, who had a year-long courtship before marriage, her experiences with relationships were casual. Ira was clear about what she wanted, and preferred her parents to find a suitable match for her. Strangely, her dad's perspective was more about getting me married than ensuring her happiness. It's frustrating when society judges, especially when she tried to be responsible.

Avni(B) married her college boyfriend, Rutuja had an arranged marriage as per her Marwari caste, and Monica's parents also found a match for her. Ankita dated multiple guys before marrying her school crush, Rohan. Despite these varied paths, my mom blames me for not finding someone yet. Mothers, with their constant opinions, can be exasperating, regardless of whether you're right or wrong.

Ira had a long-term relationship with a guy named Tushar, affectionately known as Shanti, meaning the person who rarely speaks. Despite double dating at times, she remained faithful and always sought his permission, which he graciously granted. Ira first met him during 11th-grade math coaching, where he unexpectedly offered to accompany me to a movie, "Pyaar Ke Side Effects (side effects of love)." Their friendship blossomed from there, though Shanti claims he began flirting with her from day one.

They dated on and off for nine years, causing frustration among their friends who witnessed our constant cycles of being together and apart. Ira acknowledges her immaturity during that period and the mistakes she made. However, the challenging part now is Shanti's resistance to her moving on.

Lost in thoughts of the good old days, Ira felt a wave of sleepiness wash over her. Perhaps the recent shower had contributed to her drowsiness, prompting her to decide it was time to doze off.

Day 3: 15th February 2021 – The never-ending calls

Ira was abruptly awakened by a call that felt like midnight, considering she had only just fallen asleep around 6 am after a night filled with contemplation. She knew it must be her dad calling in the morning to catch up. Seeing her dad's name on the phone, she picked up, greeted by his cheerful "GOOD MORNING!" He asked if he was interrupting her sleep, and she humorously confirmed, well aware of her jet lag.

Her dad inquired about her well-being, particularly if she had contracted any infections. They delved into a lengthy conversation about her journey from booking a hotel upon landing to the challenges faced during the flight, where she had to don coveralls, a face mask, and glasses, resembling someone prepping for surgery. She detailed the strict protocols at both Mumbai International Airport and her hotel. Her dad attentively listened, keen on every detail, expressing joy that she had tested negative for COVID-19.

Interested in her overall experience, he asked about the provided food, knowing their shared love for good meals. Ira responded that the food was okay but could have been better, resigning herself to eight more days of hotel-provided meals. As the call concluded after an hour of conversation, her dad extended his well-wishes and eagerly anticipated their in-person reunion.

After jumping out of bed, Ira hastily checked the time and was surprised to find it was already 10 am, indicating she had slept for nearly 4 hours. The exhaustion was evident; it felt as if she had been lifting heavy rocks all night. Aware that she wouldn't be able to go back to sleep, considering the barrage of calls she anticipated from concerned acquaintances, her thoughts proved accurate as her elder sister Meera was the first to call. Amused by her own whimsical imagination of ears possibly following her even here, Ira answered the call with a laugh.

A sweet and loud voice startled her, proclaiming, "Good morning." Despite a fake smile on her face, Ira managed a reply, "Morning," thinking to herself that it wasn't a good morning if you had to pretend to be happy. She wasn't mentally or emotionally prepared for the call, but she decided to be blunt, hoping her sister would stop bombarding her with questions, get annoyed, and end the call.

"Did you sleep well? Is the hotel good? How much did you spend for 10 days? Was your test negative? Why didn't Kartik drop you at the airport?" The barrage of questions from Meera seemed endless for a few minutes until Ira, sensing the need for a break, remained silent. Meera, realizing the lack of response, exclaimed, "HELLO!" Ira, grinning, cheekily replied, "Can you please breathe? You might die if you don't," adding a playful tone to the call.

Meera, unperturbed, asked, "So?" Ira, then, patiently answered the barrage of questions. She shared details about the arm guards stationed outside their room, emphasizing the strict rule of not leaving the room for 10 days. Meera, understanding the situation, commented, "Oh, okay. So, you can chill in your room, and the days will be over soon." Ira concurred, "Yeah, obviously the days will be over soon. "

During the conversation, Ira opened the door to receive her lunch, which had arrived around 12. She also spoke with her niece, Rhea, who was thrilled to see her aunt on a video call. Rhea excitedly shared all the things Ira could do in her room, providing a touch of humour to the conversation. Eventually, Ira wrapped up the call after enduring a long session of never-ending questions from her sister and niece.

A troubling thought infiltrated Ira's mind. It was a constant challenge for her to convey to others that staying alone wasn't enjoyable, especially given the struggles she had been enduring over the past year. Unable to confide in her family, she faced emotional abuse from her husband, who rarely spoke to her. He spent his days and nights playing games, recklessly spending money, and expecting to be treated like royalty—a role Ira reluctantly fulfilled. Despite her love for cooking and baking, she felt reduced to a mere maid in her own home.

While Ira enjoyed the culinary arts, her husband, like a passive observer, lounged on the sofa, consuming food like a hippo without contributing to household tasks. He never assisted with grocery shopping or even getting milk. Amid the global pandemic, when the world was grappling with the challenges of COVID-19, Ira found herself tirelessly managing household chores. She sought solace in long walks, during which she contemplated how to escape her suffocating life with someone who wasn't even a friend and treated her poorly.

Cooking became her coping mechanism, allowing her to momentarily escape from her thoughts and navigate through each day until she could find a way out. Now, in quarantine alone, she faced the very issues she had been trying to escape. It was anything but easy, despite what her elder sister believed.

From Day 4th to Day 7th, Ira found herself navigating through a fog of despondency, seeking solace in sugary treats and room service pizza. Despite the temptation, she steadfastly avoided the allure of a glass of wine, fixating on it for hours on end.

Day 8th

dawned with a glimmer of hope as Ira eagerly anticipated her impending release from quarantine and the COVID test scheduled for the morning. When the call came from reception, she practically bounded out of bed, thrilled at the prospect of human interaction. As she joined the other quarantined guests in the designated hall, a sense of camaraderie washed over her, and she greeted them with genuine smiles and warm wishes.

Instructions were given on the testing process, and as Ira struck up a conversation with a fellow guest, she learned he had recently arrived from Africa. Instantly, her anxiety spiked, her mind flooded with images from the relentless news coverage of the pandemic's impact on the continent. Apologizing hastily, she moved away, unable to shake off the fear of potential exposure.

The man, named Shashi, reassured her with a laugh, asserting his negative status. Ira responded with a half-serious, half-sarcastic remark about taking precautions, but Shashi understood the gravity of the situation, noting the discomfort of their fellow guests.

When it was finally her turn to be tested, Ira braced herself, the procedure taking a mere ten minutes before she returned to her confinement. With no symptoms to speak of, she awaited the results with cautious optimism, packing her bags in anticipation of a negative outcome. A call to her brother, Ishan, confirmed his imminent arrival for her pickup.

However, the universe had other plans. The test results arrived inconclusive, shattering Ira's hopes of imminent freedom. Anger and frustration surged within her, but she knew there was no recourse but to accept the verdict. Communicating the news to her brother, she Prioritized the safety of her elderly parents, opting to extend her stay to mitigate any potential risk.

Disheartened by her brother's casual response, Ira couldn't help but feel the weight of isolation in a world seemingly indifferent to her plight. With a heavy heart, she paid for an additional three days of isolation, dragging her burdensome luggage to her assigned room, resigned to her fate. With just three more days to go, she sighed, slipping back into her shorts and a worn-out top. In search of solace, she turned to her laptop, hoping to find something to lift her spirits.

Yet, despite her efforts, nothing seemed to go her way today. Disheartened, she closed her laptop and retreated to the window, reminiscing about the road trip she would have been on by now and the delicious home-cooked meals awaiting her after ten long days, lovingly prepared by her mother. Lost in thoughts of savory dishes and the carefree joy of mingling with people, she felt herself drifting into a drowsy haze, not from physical exhaustion, but from the sheer weariness of enduring quarantine.

Day 9th to Day 11th

Now it was hard for Ira to do anything. Let it be taking a shower, thinking about the past. Days drag by as if there is no end to it. And she is exhausted with the same thought running through her. How should she explain her parents why it didn't work? How will they take it? What will they say? What will she say? Can she tell them that they didn't have any kind of sexual relationship? Can she talk about sex to her parents? An Indian household or culture bans them from talking about it. It's not written anywhere as such, but it's unspoken, and everyone knows it. Whenever there is a romantic scene on TV or something that is seductive or sexual, parents start talking about crap things so one is distracted, or doesn't see such things. That is the kind of household she and many Indian teens have grown up in. It is considered a taboo to discuss or talk about it. And hence, the teens are more inclined towards the blue films (as in the pornographic movies) as they are banned. Kids like to do things that they are not allowed to, and hence they have no idea about what it is or how it is done. Then they try things with their so-called girlfriends without protection and end up either getting the girl pregnant or worse, with some kind of sexual disease. Even as adults they don't know how to do it or enjoy it or how to let a gal enjoy it for the least. For them, it's just what they want, as in what men want and that is it; that matters to them. They don't care about how the girl feels or if she is satisfied or not. As long as the men are satisfied, they don't really care about the women.

Saying that, even the married men hardly know about the female reproductive organ. Well, some of the sexual education is given in school, but it's just one lecture wherein no one is paying attention. All of them are either embarrassed or laughing on or against the other gender. In fabric of Indian culture, there exists a delicate web of unspoken rules and societal norms. Which is so wrong on so many levels. Sexual awakening, attraction, seduction and sex should be given more importance than anything else. It should be spoken and discussed openly in the families as it is within friends. The importance of it and the understanding of getting a new one in life or about the diseases that are deadly.

What culture are the Indians born into? From a young age, children are subtly but unmistakably made aware that certain topics are off–limits, shrouded in a veil of discomfort and embarrassment. One of the most prominent and often most stifling taboos are the discussion or rather, the lack of sexual intimacy within families. The mere mention of sexual matters can turn a conversation awkward, sending ripples of unease through the air. In many Indian households, it is not just the absence of conversations about sex but a palpable sense of avoidance and a mutable agreement to leave the topic untouched.

There is a prevailing belief that discussions about sex are unnecessary, even dangerous. Some fear that such conversations might corrupt the innocence of their children, while others worry about societal judgment. When confronted with questions or observations about sexuality, parents often resort to vague euphemisms or deflective humor, hoping to skirt the discomfort. The very thought of discussing sexual intimacy openly with one's parents can feel like a breach of an unwritten contract—a violation of the unspoken boundaries that define family relationships. As a result, many young people are left to navigate the complexities of sexual relationships without proper guidance or understanding. Myths and misconceptions about sex abound, passed from friend to friend in hushed tones. Without access to accurate information, individuals may struggle with issues of consent, reproductive health, and personal boundaries.

Breaking the silence requires courage, a willingness to confront deeply ingrained cultural norms, and perhaps most challenging of all. Oh, explaining this to her parents is going to be quite the challenge. How on earth will she even begin to broach the subject with them? That's the question weighing heaviest on Ira's mind. After pondering it for a while, she decided to approach it with strength and determination. She knew she had to do it; there was no escaping that fact. "Acceptance is key," she reminded herself, a mantra she often relied on when faced with tough situations.

Day 12th – Time to go home, the one and only place "Pune"

The awaited day had finally arrived, and Ira was bubbling with happiness and excitement, even in her thoughts. Sleep evaded her as she packed her bag with a jumble of clothes strewn around the room. Singing and dancing with joy, she anticipated her return to the safety of home.

A phone call from her dad sent her into a frenzy of excitement when he informed her that her mom would be arriving to pick her up from the hotel. "Wait at the reception," he instructed, and Ira eagerly complied. Checking and rechecking her room and belongings, she bid farewell to the space that had been her temporary abode.

Waiting at the reception, she observed the new arrivals from the government-provided bus, fresh from their airport quarantine. In her mind, she couldn't help but think, "Welcome to the ordeal, folks. These days will be worse than the pandemic itself."

Finally spotting her mom, Ira rushed over in a jolly mood, ready to embrace her. However, her mother's response was unexpected; she didn't return the hug, instead urging Ira to hurry so they could leave for Pune. Disheartened, Ira felt her excitement drain away. Perhaps her mom was tired from the journey or just hungry, she reasoned, chalking it up to "a mom thing."

Settling into the car, Ira began peppering her mom with questions about her well-being, the journey, and the traffic. When met with silence, she paused, eyeing her mother expectantly, silently willing her to respond. They hadn't seen each other for almost a year and a half, after all.

But her mom remained reticent, simply stating that everyone at home was fine. Then came the unexpected blow—why had Ira insisted on her mom making the trip? Couldn't she have just come home with the driver? It stung, the implication that her mom was inconvenienced by the pick-up.

A lone tear escaped Ira's eye as she turned towards the window, murmuring, "I'm sorry you had to come." She vowed silently that next time, she would make the journey alone. The realization that her mom didn't really want to pick her up was more disheartening than the eleven days spent in quarantine.

Recalling the conversation with her dad, who had expressed regret at not being able to make it due to work, Ira felt a pang of hurt. Here she was, her own mother speaking to her as if she were a stranger's daughter. "What a dismal start," she thought, still gazing out the window. She had been looking forward to reconnecting with people, but her mom had burst that bubble. It seemed this was just the beginning of a new chapter, a stark page turned in the book of her journey.

Busting the bubble

Despite the palpable tension that hung in the air upon her return, Ira couldn't suppress the surge of happiness within her. The journey back to Pune felt like an eternity, each passing mile filled with memories and apprehensions. Her heart raced as their destination drew near, the sight of her childhood home stirring a whirlwind of emotions.

As the familiar contours of her house came into view, Ira's mind drifted back to the last time she had stood here, bidding farewell as a newlywed embarking on the adventure of marriage. Now, returning under vastly different circumstances, she carried the weight of a truth she needed to share with her family—a truth that had kept her awake during the long nights of her journey back.

Stepping across the threshold, she was struck by the subtle changes that had taken place in her absence. The furniture seemed re-arranged, the walls adorned with new photographs. "Perhaps my parents have redecorated again," she thought wistfully, finding comfort in the familiarity tinged with novelty.

Her father's absence, away on business, left the house unusually quiet. Yash, her younger brother, was out catching up with friends, leaving Ira alone with her thoughts and the weighty suitcase that contained her life compressed into a few belongings.

With a silent resolve, she retreated to the sanctuary of her room, the door clicking shut behind her. The room felt both welcoming and alien, its contours unchanged yet subtly transformed by time. It was a place filled with memories—both joyful and bittersweet—a silent witness to the chapters of her life.

A call from her sister Meera interrupted her reverie, a brief check-in to confirm her safe arrival. "Yes, I'm here," she replied quietly before the line went dead, leaving her with her thoughts once more.

Seated on the edge of her bed, Ira allowed herself a moment of respite. The weight of the truth she carried felt almost tangible, a heavy burden that threatened to overwhelm her. "How and when do I begin unravelling this tangled web?" She wondered, her mind spinning with the possibilities and consequences of what lay ahead.

Changing into more comfortable attire, she caught a glimpse of herself in the mirror—a reflection of a woman changed by circumstance. The once vibrant glow of her youth seemed dimmed, replaced by the weariness etched into her features.

Deciding that rest was in order, Ira slipped beneath the covers, the soft embrace of her childhood bed offering a brief respite from the tumult of her thoughts. As she drifted into a fitful sleep, the events of her journey replayed in her mind like a fevered dream.

It was around 6 o'clock when she was roused from her restless slumber by the sound of her father's voice. At first, she dismissed it as a figment of her imagination, a residual echo of the days spent travelling across continents.

But as the voice persisted, growing clearer and more distinct, Ira's eyes flew open. Could it be? Was she truly home? With a surge of adrenaline, she leaped out of bed, her heart pounding in her chest.

Rushing to the door, she flung it open, her eyes scanning the hallway for any sign of her father. And there he was, seated at the dining table, a steaming cup of tea in hand.

"Did you sleep well, Beta?" He asked, his voice filled with warmth and concern. "Would you like some tea?"

The familiarity of his voice, the scent of the tea wafting through the air, brought an unexpected wave of comfort. "Yes, Papa, tea would be lovely," she replied, her voice tinged with gratitude.

As her father busied himself with the tea kettle, Ira stole a glance at her mother, who sat at the table with a stoic expression. "There is no tea," her mother remarked curtly, a hint of annoyance in her voice.

Before Ira could respond, her father intervened, a gentle smile playing on his lips. "Nonsense, let me make you a cup," he said, his tone firm yet reassuring.

Grateful for her father's intervention, Ira settled into a chair, the warmth of the tea cup cradled in her hands. The silence that followed was filled with unspoken tension, a palpable undercurrent that lingered in the air.

"How was your journey, beta?" Her father asked, breaking the silence. "Tell me everything."

And so, Ira began to recount the trials and tribulations of her journey—from the stringent protocols at London's airport to the chaotic flight on AIR INDIA. She spoke of the noisy seatmates, the long queues, and the endless wait for COVID test results.

Her father listened intently, his brow furrowing with each new revelation. The exorbitant fees for multiple COVID tests due to flight cancellations elicited a gasp of disbelief from him, a flicker of concern in his eyes.

As she sipped her tea and nibbled on a biscuit, Ira painted a vivid picture of her quarantine experience—a lone traveller in a foreign land, confined by strict rules and regulations. She spoke of the absurdity of wearing a mask to open a door, the meagre meals served on disposable plates, and the daily check-ins from masked doctors.

Through it all, her father listened, his expression a mix of empathy and astonishment. "You've been through so much," he murmured, his voice tinged with gratitude and concern.

And so, they sat in the quiet of the dining room, the ticking of the clock marking the passage of time. With each story shared, Ira felt a weight lift from her shoulders, a sense of relief mingling with the lingering apprehension.

As the afternoon waned into evening, Ira found herself enveloped in a cocoon of warmth and familiarity. The simple act of sharing tea and biscuits with her father offered a brief respite from the uncertainties that awaited her.

And in that moment, as she sat in the comforting glow of her childhood home, Ira allowed herself to believe that perhaps, just perhaps, everything would be alright.

After conversing with her father for nearly an hour, Ira felt a newfound sense of ease, able to express herself as freely as she once did. She had never anticipated that silence would come to envelop her life to such an extent that speaking would become a forgotten art.

As she sat at the dinner table with her family, Ira couldn't shake the feeling that one day had slipped away, leaving behind a lifetime of moments yet to unfold. The warmth of home and the laughter of her loved ones enveloped her, but beneath the surface, a secret weighed heavy on her mind.

It was a secret that only her sister knew, shared in text messages, unable to express her sadness in spoken words, Ira poured her heart out in the text messages, each word a piece of her soul laid bare. She told her sister of the struggles she faced, the fears that kept her awake at night, and the burden of the secret she carried. With trembling fingers, she hit send on the final message, a silent prayer on her lips. The weight lifted ever so slightly from her chest as she waited for a response, knowing that she no longer had to bear this burden alone.

She had attempted to broach the subject with her younger brother earlier, hoping he might understand. But his response, though well-intentioned, had missed the mark entirely. "Oh, so it's just about sex, right? We can go to a sexologist; he will explain," he had said, his words falling flat.

Ira sighed inwardly, realizing that her brother, like many others, couldn't comprehend the complexity of her feelings. In that moment, she resigned herself to the fact that some things were simply beyond explanation, especially to a man who had never walked in her shoes.

With a wistful smile, Ira continued to share in the family's laughter and chatter, cherishing these moments of normalcy before the weight of her secret bore down on her once more. She knew that when the time came to reveal her truth, she would do so with courage and conviction, even if it meant facing misunderstanding and uncertainty.

For now, she savoured the simple joys of family dinners and the comfort of familiar faces, knowing that she would always have their love and support, no matter what lay ahead. And as the night deepened, Ira whispered a silent prayer for strength, readying herself for the journey of a lifetime—one day gone and forever to go.

The next day, Ira's father called out to her, rousing her from her sleep. "Ira, come out; we need to talk," he said. She knew this moment had arrived, so she leaped out of bed and stood before the mirror. Brushing her hair, she looked at herself with determination and resolve.

"It's time, Ira," she whispered to herself, adopting a pose she had read about in a book. Hands on her waist, chest out like a superhero, she stood there, drawing strength from within. The mirror reflected back a woman ready to face whatever came her way.

After a few minutes of silent contemplation, she opened the door and walked out to the table where her father awaited her. "So, how do you think we should go about it, Ira? What do you think we should do?" Her father asked, the words hanging in the air. Ira was puzzled, her mind racing to grasp the meaning behind his words. "Huh... what? What is he talking about?" She thought, the confusion evident on her face.

Her father tried again, this time from a different angle. "Go to your in-laws' and get your jewellery. Tell them it's for your friend's wedding, check everything twice, and maybe take your mom with you," he explained. Still trying to make sense of it all, Ira nodded mechanically, like a puppet on strings. But before she could fully process his words, her father continued, bringing her back to the present.

"Get your jewellery. We must all visit your in-laws and talk about your marriage. Tell them it's not working. Then, we'll hire a lawyer and file for a divorce," he announced, his words hitting Ira like a ton of bricks. Shock washed over her as the reality of the situation sank in. This was it. The decision she had been agonizing over, the secret she had kept buried within her, was now out in the open. But it wasn't how she had imagined it would be.

She wanted to discuss what had happened, to explain the pain, the tears, and the fears that had led her to this point. Yet here she was, confronted with a plan laid out for her, as if it were a simple task to check off a list. Relief mingled with a profound sense of emptiness in Ira's heart. Her parents didn't want to know the details, didn't want to delve into the depths of her suffering. It was as if her pain meant nothing, as if the one and a half years of her life had been erased with a few words. How could this be? How could her own mother, who knew her pain, not ask a single question? The ache in her chest grew as she realized the depth of her isolation, the silence that enveloped her pain.

She had barely confided in her sister, sending just one long message that hardly scratched the surface of her turmoil. But now, faced with the reality of her parents' decision, she felt the weight of her loneliness like a physical ache. "What the hell is happening?" She thought, her mind reeling with disbelief. She pinched herself, feeling the sharp pain, confirming that this was indeed her reality. The pain was real, the situation undeniable. Ira stood there, her heart heavy with the weight of unspoken words, wondering how life could unravel so swiftly, leaving her stranded in a sea of unanswered questions and unspoken pain.

With a determined nod, Ira stood up from the table and announced, "Yes, I shall visit my in-laws and take Mom with me today itself." She left the table, her mind racing with thoughts of what lay ahead. Opening her bag, she carefully selected her outfit for the day. She took a shower, the water washing away the lingering traces of doubt and fear. As she got ready, she felt a sense of resolve settling over her. Around 11 o'clock, Ira and her mom stepped out of the house, the air heavy with unspoken tension. The ride to Borarwake's house was filled with silence, each passing moment stretching like an eternity.

Her mom sat beside her, silent as ever, and Ira couldn't help but feel a surge of frustration. "Your daughter is suffering; what the hell is wrong with you?" she wanted to scream. "Don't you want to know what happened? Don't you want to yell at me for letting this happen?" But her mother remained silent, like a ghost of the past, haunting the present with her absence of words. Ira seethed with anger, the weight of her mother's indifference bearing down on her.

Finally, they reached her in-laws' house, and Ira's mother-in-law came running outside at the sight of her. It had been one and a half years since they had seen each other, and her mother-in-law's genuine happiness was palpable. She enveloped Ira in a warm hug, inviting her inside. The sun shone brightly, casting a surreal glow over the scene. Her mother-in-law was excited, bombarding her with questions about her "navra" (husband in Marathi).

"He is good, just working from home," Ira replied, her voice sounding distant even to her own ears. Her mother-in-law and father-in-law spoke animatedly, their chatter filling the room. With a forced smile on her face, Ira answered their questions, all the while feeling the weight of the impending conversation. She ate the food her mother-in-law had prepared, each bite a bitter reminder of the charade she was playing. "Please don't ask me questions; please do not feed me," she thought desperately, knowing that none of this would change her decision. She knew that once she told her in-laws about the divorce, they would have questions, questions that her own parents hadn't asked.

As she chewed on a samosa, her mind raced with thoughts of escape. "Don't try to blackmail me with good behaviour," she wanted to scream. "I won't stay with your son just because you're being nice now." After a meal that seemed to stretch on forever, filled with samosas, cakes, juices, and tea, Ira finally mustered the courage to bring up the reason for her visit.

"My best friend is getting married, as I told you before I came. I need the jewellery that I can wear for the wedding," she said, her voice steady despite the turmoil inside. Her mother-in-law got up eagerly, disappearing into another room to retrieve the jewellery. She returned with a box, explaining how her father-in-law had retrieved it from the bank locker that very morning. Ira opened the box, her heart pounding in her chest. She checked each piece, finding everything in place. With a sense of relief washing over her, she bid goodbye to her in-laws, promising to return to stay with them for a few days after the wedding.

As she stepped out of the house, the weight of the jewellery box in her hand, Ira couldn't shake the feeling of unease. The conversations she had avoided, the questions left unanswered, all lingered in the air around her. But for now, she focused on the task at hand, steeling herself for the road ahead. With each step away from her in-laws' house, she felt a sense of liberation, a glimmer of hope amidst the chaos of her unravelling life.

As the car rolled along the familiar streets, Ira was enveloped in a whirlwind of thoughts that seemed to suffocate her. The jewellery box sat heavy in her lap, a stark reminder of the charade she had just endured.

"Is the jewellery so important that you guys don't want to talk about me and what I have been through?" She thought bitterly, her heart heavy with disappointment.

The year 2020 had brought the world to its knees with the pandemic, with people dying of COVID-19 and lives upturned in unimaginable ways. Yet, for Ira, the pandemic was just one layer of her suffering.

Living with a man who hardly spoke to her, who treated her more like a maid than a wife, had been its own kind of hell. Weekends were spent cleaning the house from top to bottom, and preparing meals from dawn till dusk, all while her husband retreated into the world of his PS4.

They didn't even share a room, sleeping in separate spaces as if they were strangers inhabiting the same house. The silence between them was deafening, a constant reminder of the emptiness that had seeped into their marriage.

Ira felt like she was drowning in a sea of unspoken words, her heart aching for the emotional connection that had long since vanished. Her husband, wrapped up in his own world, seemed oblivious to her pain, content to live in the confines of his virtual reality.

And now, her parents' behaviour only added to her sense of isolation. It was as if she was a task to be completed, an item on their to-do list that needed to be checked off. The focus was solely on retrieving the jewellery, the expensive 500 grams of gold that had been given to her. "Yes, she understands it's valuable," Ira muttered to herself, her frustration bubbling to the surface. "But was this the time to bring it up? Couldn't they see that I needed their emotional support more than ever?"

Tears welled up in her eyes, a mixture of anger and sadness threatening to spill over. This was not the reaction she had expected from her parents, the ones she had always turned to in times of need.

"All they wanted was the jewellery back," she thought bitterly, feeling the weight of their indifference like a physical ache. "As if I'm just their friend's kid, and my suffering doesn't really have an impact on them." The car ride seemed endless, each passing moment filled with a suffocating silence. Ira longed to scream, to unleash the pent-up emotions that threatened to consume her.

But instead, she sat there in silence, the weight of her disappointment pressing down on her like a leaden weight. As the car pulled into the driveway of her home, Ira took a deep breath, steeling herself for the conversations that lay ahead. She knew that she couldn't continue living this way, suffocating in a marriage devoid of love and understanding. It was time to take control of her own life, to stand up for herself and demand the happiness she deserved.

With a newfound sense of determination, Ira stepped out of the car, the jewellery box clutched tightly in her hand. The journey ahead would be difficult, but she was ready to face it head-on. For now, she would confront her parents, demand the emotional support she needed, and begin the process of untangling herself from a marriage that had become a prison. But she knew that she wouldn't be able to confront her parents anytime soon.

Thunder – the awakening

Thunder rumbled in the distance, a deep, Primal sound that seemed to echo the tumultuous emotions raging within Ira. As she stood in her room, the jewellery box heavy in her hands, the storm outside mirrored the tempest swirling inside her. Each roll of thunder was like a drumbeat, a call to awaken from the numbness that had settled over her life. The silence of the house was broken by the roar of the storm, a stark contrast to the suffocating silence of her marriage. With steady hands, she opened the jewellery box and placed it on her dresser. Its gleaming contents seemed to mock her a symbol of the life she had been forced to live.

But no more.

With a resolute gesture, Ira removed her wedding ring and placed it beside the jewellery box. The sound of thunder seemed too crescendo around her, urging her on. "I will not be bound by this anymore," she whispered to the storm, her voice barely audible over the roar of the thunder.

With a deep breath, she left her room, the storm raging outside matching the turmoil in her heart. Outside, her parents awaited her, unaware of the awakening that was about to unfold. As she entered the living room, the air crackling with tension, Ira felt a surge of power. She stood tall, her chin lifted defiantly, ready to face whatever came her way. She knew that she was ready to reclaim her life, to break free from the chains of silence and indifference.

The storm outside raged on, but inside Ira, a new resolve burned bright. She was thunderous - fierce, unstoppable, and ready to awaken to a new beginning. But she was still not up to confess her parents to ask for emotional support. She was always a gal who found it hard to ask for help, no matter how much she would be killing herself in the process. But her parents didn't think of what was required in this situation, which made her feel isolated with her pain.

The ringing phone broke the silence of Ira's thoughts, and a smile immediately graced her lips when she saw Shruti's name flashing on the screen. Shruti, her best friend, the one person who knew the entire story from its inception to its current twisted versions. Answering the call, Ira was greeted by Shruti's cheerful voice on the other end. "Hey Ira, how are you doing? I bet you must be enjoying some good food after those hellish days you suffered in quarantine," Avni exclaimed.

Forcing a smile, Ira replied, "Yes, trying to." But before Avni could dive into the usual banter, Ira spilled everything that had transpired since her return home. Avni listened intently, her disbelief evident in the silence that followed.

Avni understood the depths of her parents' negligence, their failure to ask about the turmoil Ira had been enduring. With a firm yet gentle voice, Avni encouraged Ira to stay strong, to speak her truth without letting emotions cloud her words.

"You're on the right path, Ira. You need to confront your parents," Avni advised, her words a soothing balm to Ira's frayed nerves. With tears in her eyes, Ira nodded, thanking Avni for being the unwavering pillar of support she needed. The call ended with some light-hearted jokes and shared laughter, leaving Ira feeling a sense of relief wash over her.

After hanging up, Ira couldn't stop smiling at the thought of her friendship with Shruti. It had all started back in August 2014 when she and her friend Rupali, fondly known as Mau, had joined a spinning class at Endurance gym.

Soon, a close-knit gang was formed, including Avni (Shru), Isha (Ishu), and Arohi (Aru). They became known as the "gang of 5 gals" at the gym, spending hours chatting in the parking lot after their spinning sessions. People often wondered what they talked about every day, but the gang didn't care. They found solace and camaraderie in each other's company, forging bonds that would last a lifetime.

Fast forward to 2021, and they knew each other's pain, and understood each other's struggles to the depths of the ocean. Ira cherished these friendships, knowing they were her lifelines in times of need.

She recalled a moment in 2020 when she was living in London with her husband, and he had demanded money from her. It was then that she had confided in Shruti, adamant that she wouldn't call her dad for money.

To her surprise, it was Avni and her husband, Namish, who had stepped up without hesitation, offering to help her out. It was a gesture that touched Ira deeply, showing her the unwavering trust and support they had for her.

In that moment, Ira realized how lucky she was to have found Shruti, a friend and advisor who had always been there for her. She made a silent vow to herself that she would always be there for them in return, no matter what life threw their way.

The new day dawned with a weight of complications, isolation, and an undercurrent of sadness that seemed to envelop Ira. Today, she was set to face a meeting with her sister Meera and her brother-in-law Parth, joined by the rest of the family.

Sitting around the table, Ira's heart raced with anticipation of the conversation that was about to unfold. The whole family was there, gathered to discuss the next steps in her journey towards liberation.

However, her niece, the ever-curious and smart 6-year-old, was left out of the serious discussion, her innocence shielded from the sombre atmosphere.

The meeting commenced with discussions on how to approach the impending conversation with Ira's in-laws. Her father, with a sense of authority, asked Parth and Meera to stand by her side during this crucial moment.

Without wasting any time, Ira's father picked up the phone and dialled Mr Sarthak, her father-in-law, informing him of their intention to visit on Thursday for a serious discussion. The timing was set, and the wheels were set in motion.

As the discussion continued, Meera suggested the name of a family friend who was a lawyer, emphasizing his expertise in handling such cases. Ira's father, nodding in agreement, saw the wisdom in this suggestion and accepted it without hesitation. The room was filled with a mix of emotions—determination, apprehension, and a glimmer of hope. With the meeting adjourned, and the plans set, Ira couldn't help but feel a sense of relief mingled with nervous anticipation. The road ahead was uncertain, but she knew she had her family beside her, ready to face whatever challenges came their way.

As she sat alone in her room later that evening, the weight of the day's discussions settled over her. But amidst the turmoil, a flicker of hope burned bright within her heart. With a deep breath, Ira steeled herself for the days to come. She was ready to confront her truth, to break free from the chains of a loveless marriage, and to reclaim her life with courage and determination. The journey ahead would be tough, and she knew she was alone in it, as her own family was standing in the stadium just to watch her without any empathy towards her.

The Rat Race

Thursday morning felt like every other day spent with her husband—dull and draining. Ira rose and readied herself in silence, conserving her energy for the upcoming ordeal. Soon, Meera and Parth arrived, and everyone set off for Mr Sarthak's house. In the car, her father launched into a lengthy lecture about how Ira hadn't heeded his warnings against marrying this man, predicting the suffering that would follow. Despite her anger simmering beneath the surface, she listened as her father recounted everything from her school days to her job choices, all leading to the man she had married.

No one could decipher Ira's thoughts at that moment. Upon reaching her in-laws' house, her mother-in-law's excitement was palpable, expecting good news—perhaps Ira was pregnant. She hugged Ira and rushed inside, thoroughly delighted. Inviting everyone in, after the obligatory weather and general discussions, Ira's father cleared his throat and subtly nudged her to speak up.

Ira glanced around at the room filled with family and her in-laws, gathering her resolve before beginning to address the room. "It's not working," she said firmly, her voice carrying weight. "Kartik and I are just coexisting like flatmates who hardly speak to one another. It's been over a year, yet we haven't had a husband-wife relationship."

As these words spilled out, a stunned silence enveloped the room. Her mother-in-law gasped, "Are you serious? Not even once?" Ira shook her head. "No, in fact, we don't even share a room. Kartik constantly complains of back pain, needing more space, insisting I stay in another room for a while."

Since their marriage, sharing a room had become a rarity, with Kartik citing his ongoing pain whenever Ira broached the subject. "Whenever I ask to shift back to our room," she continued, "Kartik claims he still needs time to recover."

Her mother-in-law, unable to contain her curiosity, then inquired about their honeymoon. Ira couldn't help but grin, launching into the recount of their time in Goa, their honeymoon destination.

"The first day was uneventful, just the journey," Ira reminisced. "The following day, I suggested we go for a couple's spa, but Kartik denied the idea. Later, when he went out to buy slippers for the beach, I suggested we get them from the resort, but he insisted on going outside." She recalled the secluded Caravela Beach Resort, a considerable distance from the market. "Despite my offer to accompany him, he refused, booking a cab and leaving me alone in the room for the entire morning."

"As we dined that evening," Ira continued, "Kartik remained engrossed in conversation with the chef about the food. When I reminded him, we were on our honeymoon and asked him to talk to me instead, he simply brushed me off, telling me to use my phone."

Frustration simmered within her, wondering if her marriage was a mistake or if Kartik had simply lost interest. Determined to spark some connection, she recalled a conversation with friends about seduction.

"Next morning, after showering, I emerged in a towel, engaging him in idle chatter as I applied lotion," Ira recounted. "I thought I'd try something new, but to my disbelief, he remained completely indifferent."

Undeterred, she suggested they visit the resort's pool and bar. "Finally," she sighed in relief, "he agreed." Ira quickly changed into her swimming costume and a short dress, ready for a hopeful moment of connection.

However, her hopes were dashed when Kartik settled on a pool bench with his laptop and beer, refusing to join her in the water. "Furious," Ira recalled, "I left him in anger, ordering a whisky on ice to cool down before immersing myself in the pool."

Lost in her memories, Ira pondered the reasons behind Kartik's behaviour. "I spent hours in the pool, racking my brains," she continued. "Maybe he preferred subtlety, or perhaps he had a girlfriend, or maybe..." Her thoughts trailed off.

Then, a call from the reception for Kartik interrupted her thoughts. Confused, she accepted the call, only for Kartik to pass the phone to her, saying the receptionist wanted to speak to his wife. "It turns out," Ira recounted, "they offered to arrange a private beach dinner for us, just the two of us, with music and good food."

Eager for any sign of connection, Ira agreed, hoping it might bridge the gap between them. However, the evening turned out to be a disaster, with Kartik complaining about everything from the food to the weather, showing no appreciation for her efforts.

"That was the worst evening of my life," Ira admitted, her voice heavy with disappointment. "I realized something was seriously wrong when, in my frustration, I finally asked him why he was so distant, why he hadn't made any effort during our entire trip."

To her astonishment, Kartik replied, "Oh no, Ira, this isn't our honeymoon. We're here to relax after all the wedding craziness."

The weight of his words hit her like a ton of bricks, leaving Ira shattered and confused. "This is not our honeymoon," she repeated, feeling a deep sense of betrayal and sadness wash over her.

As she finished recounting her tale, Ira felt a heavy silence settle over the room. Her family and in-laws listened intently, the gravity of her words sinking in. Her sister and brother-in-law, Meera and Parth, stared at her with a mix of shock and sorrow, silently offering their support.

Unable to meet their eyes, Ira stared at the floor, feeling the weight of her experiences bearing down on her. Her family had never asked about her struggles, unaware of the turmoil she had endured.

The room fell into a sober silence, the unspoken pain and disappointment hanging heavy in the air as Ira's story echoed in their minds.

Still, her mother-in-law persisted, eager to hear about Ira's experiences in London. Ira glanced around at the expectant faces and began recounting her lonely journey despite being married.

"After we arrived in London on December 20th, 2019, the cold hit us hard, as it should in December," Ira started. "Both of us were suffering from cold and cough due to the drastic weather change from 30 degrees in Pune to 5 degrees in London."

Upon reaching their London home, Kartik wasted no time in his peculiar behaviour. He said, “You have a cold, and I don’t want to get sick. Why don’t you sleep on the couch?'" Ira recalled the memory, still fresh in her mind. "On the very first day, I knew it was going to be tough. Without my agreement, Kartik fetched the cushion and cover for the couch, making me sleep in the living room."

She continued, detailing the days that followed. "After a couple of days, I shifted to his room, but it was short-lived. Soon, Kartik began complaining about his back pain, insisting that I sleep in the other room." Ira's voice betrayed a hint of resignation. "I didn’t argue. I simply took the blanket and moved to the other room. The days dragged on, with us not sharing a room, growing more distant."

Turning to her mother-in-law, Ira expressed her frustration. "I told her that Kartik didn’t care for me at all, treating me like a maid." She shook her head, the disappointment evident in her expression. "We didn’t have any physical relationship. We didn’t even hug."

As she neared the end of her tale, Ira revealed a heartbreaking detail. "The first time he hugged me was when I was boarding my taxi to the airport, after 1 year and 20 days of our marriage," she said, her voice tinged with sadness. "He didn’t even accompany me to the airport."

The room descended into a weighty silence as Ira concluded her narrative, her words hanging in the air with palpable gravity. Her mother-in-law listened attentively, seeming to grasp the profound depths of Ira's solitude and disillusionment within her marriage.

In the ensuing quiet, no one dared to break the stillness. They all gazed into nothingness, and inexplicably, tears welled up in Ira's eyes. She realized she had exhausted every effort to confront the situation, yet nothing had yielded results. Unable to stem the flow of tears, she allowed them to fall, a release that felt like the unlocking of the silence she carried within. It was a bittersweet relief.

After what seemed like an eternity, Ira's father spoke up, "So, this is the situation. I don't believe it can continue. My daughter has given her all and suffered greatly. Let's end it here and allow her the life she deserves—the happiness she deserves." The weight of his words settled heavily in the room.

As Ira listened to her father, a part of her wanted to brush it off, to hush it over. Little did she know that this was just the beginning—the erosion of her soul, slowly breaking her into pieces.

Taking Ira aside, her mother-in-law asked for a detailed account of what had transpired. When Ira recounted the ordeal once more, her mother-in-law couldn't contain her tears. "I'll speak to Kartik. It will work out; please don't ask for a divorce. What will happen to the family? Everyone will be heartbroken, my family as well as his," she pleaded.

But Ira, with a resolute tone, replied, "I'm sorry, but I can't endure this any longer. I've been suffering every day for the past year. While you spoke to him every other weekend, he always had a false explanation. He refuses to acknowledge anything." She recounted how even her elder sister had spoken to him, yet he remained obstinate.

"If that's the case, it doesn't make sense to stay," she concluded, rising from her seat and leaving the room without a backward glance. Stepping out of the room, Ira addressed her father, "Papa, let's go." Her family rose in unison, wordlessly acknowledging her decision. They left the house without a word, each lost in their thoughts. As the cars pulled out of the driveway and onto the familiar road where she was brought as a bride, Ira couldn't help but reminisce about that day. The stark contrast between then and now was overwhelming, and she found herself staring blankly at the road ahead, her mind devoid of any thoughts.

After coming back home, no one said anything, and Ira went back to her room to her cocoon to sit and relax a bit after the explosion that she had felt in her in-laws' house. The remaining day was just a drag. She had food and slept almost all of the remaining day. She was tired mentally and emotionally and required to rest and not talk to anyone. Her parents, who never dared to ask her anything had listened to her side of the story the 1st time, and they thought okay, like that's it. They didn't know the details of it; no one knew except her bff's as they were the ones who stood by her when she was going through a hard time. Mentally they gave her the strength and were there with her when no one was.

The following morning, Ira's father called her out, informing her that they needed to find a lawyer. He mentioned having spoken with Meera, who's relative was a lawyer known for handling cases like theirs. Trusting Meera's judgment, both Ira and her father went to meet this lawyer, Mrs Gupta.

Once inside Mrs Gupta's office, she respectfully asked Ira's father to wait outside, understanding that Ira might find it uncomfortable to discuss personal matters in his presence. It felt right to have this Private conversation. After what seemed like an hour, Ira's father was called back in, and the three of them began discussing the situation.

Mrs Gupta advised Ira's father to contact her father-in-law (FIL) to discuss the next steps. However, Ira interjected, suggesting that the lawyer should make the call instead. She explained that her FIL tended to talk a lot, even on regular days, which could complicate matters. Mrs Gupta disagreed, insisting that Ira should speak to him politely to expedite the divorce proceedings.

Reluctantly, Ira's father agreed and called her FIL. As expected, he launched into a lengthy monologue about saving the marriage and how Ira should reconsider. He even mentioned that Kartik was willing to accept her despite everything.

This infuriated Ira's father, who pointed out that it was Kartik's actions causing the turmoil, not Ira's. He refused to let her be blamed and emphasized that Ira was resolute in seeking a divorce, regardless of what Kartik claimed.

The call ended abruptly, with Ira's father frustrated at her FIL's words. Observing this exchange, Ira decided to take charge. She told Mrs Gupta that she should handle the case herself, not wanting to burden her father further. After all, what was the point of a lawyer if her father had to do all the work?

Unexpectedly, Ira's father scolded her in front of Mrs Gupta, insisting she show respect, as Mrs Gupta was Meera's relative and knew what was best. This unexpected reprimand left Ira stunned.

Feeling overwhelmed and unwilling to argue with her father in front of a stranger, Ira excused herself from the room. She had only shared her thoughts, but her father seemed intent on making it seem like she was at fault. This frustration added to her already heavy burden. She left, not wanting to bad-mouth anyone unnecessarily. Ira couldn't help but feel a pang of hurt. She wished her father would take her side for once, acknowledging the suffering she had endured. Instead, it seemed like her dad was more concerned about appearances in front of Meera's in-laws, leaving Ira feeling even more alone in her struggle.

The first meeting with the lawyer left both Ira and her father drained. On the way back home, they avoided eye contact, each lost in their own thoughts. Her father felt Ira had disrespected the lawyer, who was also Meera's relative. Ira, on the other hand, believed personal feelings should be set aside when seeking professional help, especially since they were paying for the service.

Back home, a tense conference unfolded around the dining table with Ira, her father, mother, and her brother Ishan. Her father began raising his voice, insisting that Ira needed to control her anger, watch her words, and show respect as Mrs Gupta had advised. He suggested that perhaps her behaviour and anger had contributed to her failed marriage. Since Meera had recommended the lawyer, who happened to be her relative, her father warned that if Ira didn't behave appropriately, Meera might suffer the consequences.

Feeling the need to express herself, Ira spoke softly, trying to explain to her father the importance of letting the lawyer handle certain aspects, not him. She emphasized that dealing with her father-in-law directly could lead to more complications, especially given his tendency to push back and speak ill of her. She explained that emotions were running high, and involving everyone directly might escalate into unnecessary conflicts.

But her father had a different viewpoint. He insisted that they should follow Mrs Gupta's advice since she was Meera's relative and deserved respect. Ira struggled to contain her frustration, and finally, unable to hold back, she stood up and exclaimed, "Papa, we are here to solve my problem, not to please your other daughter. Focus on me for now, and you can tend to her in-laws later."

With tears of anger and hurt in her eyes, Ira left the room, feeling overwhelmed by her father's inability to see what was right for her. No matter what she did, she always felt compared to her sister. In this critical situation, it seemed her father was favouring Meera, the elder daughter, when Ira needed his support the most.

Ira found herself in a sea of troubles, longing only for peace and quiet. She reasoned that letting Mrs Gupta handle the legal matters might ease tensions with her father, who would eventually realize she wasn't the best fit for the job. So, she conceded, stepping out to reconcile with her father and agreeing to Mrs Gupta's representation. But this respite was short-lived.

With each passing day, matters grew more fraught. Mrs Gupta urged her father to contact her in-laws regarding divorce proceedings, but he hesitated, feeling it wasn't his responsibility. Eventually, he relented, calling her father-in-law, who, in a fit of anger, suggested Ira try again with his son. This infuriated Ira, who retorted that her husband's shortcomings weren't hers to bear, and she refused to sacrifice more time and happiness.

Her father, unable to grasp her perspective, questioned if she would return to her husband. Defiantly, she declined, leaving to find solace elsewhere. In a mix of frustration and anguish, she sought refuge in a bar, reaching out to a friend for companionship. Jyoti arrived, understanding Ira's need for silence, offering her presence without words.

In that quiet camaraderie, Ira realized the depth of Jyoti's friendship, grateful for her understanding in her time of need.

The Stretch

It was April 2021 when Ira met the lawyer and decided to file for divorce. She thought it would be done within six months, as it was a mutual decision, but this was India, and nothing was easy when it came to the courts. Three months had passed, and her so-called husband hadn't called her once since she had met his parents. Not that Ira expected anything from that jerk. Still, she had harboured a faint hope that he would show some maturity and understand the gravity of the situation, but that hope had long since dissipated.

Her father-in-law's words echoed in her mind: "He is ready to accept you even after all you have done." The phrase had lodged itself in her brain, impossible to dislodge. Maybe his parents were forcing him to say it. Maybe the marriage had been a scam all along. Ira knew she was a hopeless romantic, influenced by the books she read, the poems she wrote, and the movies that inspired her. She never imagined she would fall head over heels in every relationship she had.

During her university days, Ira dated and had a boyfriend who treated her well, respected her choices, and believed in her. Back in

2009, when she was in the 11th grade, she had joined a class with her school friend Rutuja for Math and Science, as she was weak in these subjects. She remembered those days fondly as she sat on her bed, lost in thoughts while a movie played on her laptop. She was a big fan of movies, especially romantic and fiction genres. It was Rutuja who introduced her to "Twilight," starring Robert Pattinson as Edward Cullen and Kristen Stewart as Bella Swan. When Rutuja told her the book was even better than the movie, Ira bought her first book. That was how she started reading. The more she read, the more she aspired to be a better person and to find an everlasting partner who would love her for who she was.

When she met Tushar, she wasn't looking for a boyfriend. She just wanted to have fun and enjoy life. But Tushar pursued her persistently until she gave in, thinking, what harm could it do? Ira was short-tempered, just like her dad, which led to numerous breakups with Tushar. But he knew her well and understood that she would always come back to him, no matter how angry she got. They spent their time together watching movies, holding hands, and going on long rides on his bike. Even when Ira went to London for further studies, they maintained a long-distance relationship, staying faithful and communicating a lot to avoid misunderstandings.

In November 2015, when Ira returned from London, Tushar proposed to her. She told him to convince his mother, who disliked Ira, thinking she was too arrogant and assertive. Ira knew from the beginning that she wouldn't ask Tushar to choose between her and his mother. It was too cruel. Tushar was from Jalgaon, and he had come to Pune for better educational opportunities. He returned to Jalgaon to convince his mother, who was staunchly against their marriage. Ira thought his mother just needed time to accept the relationship, believing Tushar would never leave her after being together for over nine years.

But in 2016, Tushar went back to Jalgaon for summer vacation. At a later reunion, he introduced everyone to his wife, Priyanka. Ira, late to the party due to work, was shocked and heartbroken when she received the news. Yet, she attended the reunion, walked straight up to Tushar and his wife, and introduced herself as one of Tushar's best friends, even hugging Priyanka. Tushar had expected her to avoid the reunion, but he realized he didn't know her at all, even after nine years. Ira faced challenges head-on, bolstering herself with motivational speeches and courage. She didn't cry or show sadness as her friends had anticipated. Instead, she had a few drinks, danced, and enjoyed herself, as usual.

Seeing Ira so composed, Tushar was bewildered. He caused a scene, questioning how she could be so normal. Rutuja sarcastically remarked, "You definitely don't know her. Maybe that's why you'll spend eternity wondering why you didn't marry her." Overhearing this, Ira laughed, high-fived Rutuja, and said, "Bang on!" She grinned, reflecting on the memory, and reassured herself that, just as she had moved on from a nine-year relationship, she would soon be free from her brief, unhappy marriage.

Ira was getting ready to meet her lawyer for a one-on-one session. She needed to know the details of her case, and yet, her father accompanied her to the office. Mrs Gupta, the lawyer, told him to wait outside while Ira settled comfortably on the couch with a cup of steaming hot coffee in her hand.

After a short while, Mrs Gupta began, "There are a few things I need to know about your relationship with Kartik. Is there anything you'd like to share?"

Ira felt blank and replied, "You can ask your questions to get the exact information you need, and I will answer them."

So began the long line of questions:

1. When did you get married?

- "I had a court marriage on May 8th, 2019, for visa purposes since Kartik lived in London. Our wedding ceremony was on December 9th, 2019."

2. Did you go for a honeymoon? And if yes, did you notice any difference in his behaviour?

- "Oh, yeah!" Ira exclaimed. "We went to Goa for three days, and it was the worst trip ever. On our first night, during dinner, he kept talking with the chef and manager about the food. When she complained and asked if he could focus on us for a moment, he replied, "You have your phone, right? Use it. I like talking to chefs," and left me alone. The next day, he said he forgot his slippers and insisted on going out to buy them, even though I suggested getting some from the resort reception. When I offered to accompany him, as the resort was on the outskirts and he'd be gone a while, he refused and left me alone, spending nearly the whole day away. She walked along the beach for hours, thinking maybe he was stuck on his last girlfriend or maybe he was gay. On the third day, I suggested we go for a couple's spa since it was our honeymoon. He retorted, "No, it's not. We're here to relax after all those wedding ceremonies." He went for a solo spa session, leaving me alone again. Later, she suggested swimming because it was really hot. He agreed, but when she got in the pool and turned around, there he was with his laptop and earphones, watching a movie. When she asked him to join me in the water and have a drink together, he said, "You can have your drink in the water; I'll have mine here. I don't feel like getting in the pool." At that point, she decided she was done asking him for anything. He needed to grow up and understand that as his wife, he had responsibilities toward me. She wasn't going to push it anymore.

Mrs Gupta listened in shock; her eyebrows raised. "Really? Is this what happened?" She asked, incredulous.

"Yes," Ira replied casually, "and this is just the beginning of what is to come."

3. When did you leave for London, and was there any difference in his behaviour there? Was he good to you?

"We left for London on December 20th, 2019. When we landed, the temperature was nearly 3 degrees Celsius, compared to the 30 degrees we had in India. She was suffering from a cold due to the freezing temperatures. As soon as we reached home, he offered me coffee and behaved normally. We ordered food, ate together, and watched a good movie on TV.

Later, when it was time to sleep, he said, "Ira, you're suffering from a cold, and I don't want to catch it because I have work to do. Why don't you sleep on the couch since I have to get up really early tomorrow?" Listening to that, she went numb. She had nothing to say, so she just nodded. "Within a few minutes, he brought me a cushion and a blanket for the couch."

Ira glanced at the lawyer, who was now emotional, tears silently streaming down her face as she wiped them away. Ira continued, "And that was my first day in London." She took a long sip of her coffee, avoiding eye contact with the lawyer.

4. London is well known for its Winter Wonderland and New Year's Eve celebrations. Did you go anywhere? How was your experience?

Ira thought for a moment, wondering why the lawyer was asking so many questions, when her parents didn't ask any. When would this end?

"Yes, I was excited to attend the Winter Wonderland and New Year's Eve celebrations," she replied. "I suggested we go out and enjoy the festivities. But Kartik said, 'I've seen it many times. Why don't you go out with your friends and enjoy yourself? I'm not really fond of the weather." When I asked what he would do while I was out, he replied, "I'll play games on TV. It's been a long time since I've had the chance."

"He knew I had many friends in London from my university days, which was why he decided to push me out. Whenever I later asked him to go out, whether to a museum or for the Chinese New Year celebrations, he always had the same answer. Eventually, my friends began to ask if I was having problems in my marriage. I took my husband's side, saying, 'Nah, all is good. He's just a bit of an introvert.'

But the truth was, I was trying to defend him when there was nothing he was doing for me."

Saying this, Ira glanced at Mrs Gupta, who was taking notes and listening intently. The lawyer nodded sympathetically, understanding more of Ira's struggles. Ira took a deep breath, feeling the weight of the memories but also a sense of relief in sharing them.

4. Did he introduce you to any of his friends?

- Yes, he introduced me to his friend Anand and his wife Sangeeta. They are from Mumbai and have twins. One time, I went out with Sangeeta, and she asked about my health. I told her I was fine. Then she mentioned that she and Anand missed me at the party on Friday night at his workplace. I had no idea what she was talking about. After asking a few questions, I found out that Anand and Kartik's manager had invited everyone's wives for drinks and dinner after work, and Kartik had told them I wouldn't be attending because I was unwell.

- Ira was completely unaware of this, and when she confronted Kartik, he showed no emotion and simply said, "I thought you wouldn't be interested, so I didn't ask." Hearing this, she was furious and said he should have at least mentioned it. She pointed out that now Sangeeta knows he lied, and it's his problem to fix. She left the room in despair, wondering what she did to deserve a partner like him. If Sangeeta hadn't told her, she never would have realized what Kartik was doing and would have continued losing respect for him.

5. I guess around March 2020, the pandemic hit London, United Kingdom. How was he treating you then?

- Lost in thought for a while, Mrs Gupta gave her a moment of silence to gather her thoughts. After a few deep breaths, she began another story.

- The pandemic did hit in March 2020, and more than the pandemic, she remembered the pain she went through. Kartik started working from home, like many others around the world. Ira thought she would get more time to spend with him and understand him better, but that turned out to be another false hope.

- The sleeping situation remained mostly the same. Now, she was sleeping in one room and he in another. They had slept together in the same room for maybe a week before Kartik told Ira he couldn't sleep because of back pain and needed more space. He said he had a habit of tossing and turning all night and needed her to sleep in another room until he recovered. Ira had long given up on arguing, so she started living in another room. He was indeed the worst flatmate ever.

- During the pandemic, London was in complete lockdown for the first two weeks. Then, Mr Boris Johnson allowed two hours of outdoor exercise in the morning and opened shops for two hours in the morning and evening. Ira thought that since Kartik was working from home, he would go grocery shopping with her, and they could have a somewhat normal life. But there was no such thing as normal with Kartik. Staying in the house all day, he would eat all the food that Ira cooked. She was making Indian delicacies she had never made before, as if she were feeding twenty people. He would eat everything she prepared, leaving nothing for her. She would often starve, too tired to cook again, and preferred to just lie down. To reduce the stress, she started going for long walks and runs. She called her best friends and talked about her suffering, but there seemed to be no end to it.

- Ira remembered one incident so well that it still gave her chills. Kartik asked her to make samosas, something she had never made before. She found a recipe on YouTube and started the process. While deep frying the samosas, she burned her chest. Kartik heard her yell in pain but was least bothered. She finished making the samosas and chutney, placed them in front of him, and sat beside him on the couch with an ice pack on her chest. Without asking anything about her burn, he continued eating the samosas while Ira quivered in pain. He didn't even offer to get a cream from the medical store. That was when she knew it was over and that she needed to get out of this situation as soon as the world reopened.

6. Did he ever cook for you?

- Yes, he did. He liked to make pasta and occasionally cooked it for her, but he left the kitchen a mess, and I had to clean it up. He used the utensils as if he had hired a maid, leaving the cleaning to me. Kartik loved Biryani and often asked me to make it. He thought making Chicken Biryani was very simple and didn't take much time, accusing me of complaining for no reason. To prove a point, I gave him a recipe and had him make the Biryani he loved. By the time it was ready, I had fallen asleep from hunger. He had burnt the Biryani, but I still appreciated his effort. However, he never appreciated my efforts for Biryani or anything else for that matter.

7. Did you ever tell your parents about anything?

- "I couldn't," claimed Ira. "I just couldn't. It was the pandemic already. So many people were dying, and the world was suffering. I didn't want my parents to suffer more than they had to.

- Moreover, they had told me not to marry this guy, and I insisted I would. I remember my dad saying, 'Don't marry Kartik; he is not the guy for you.' When I asked him for a reason, he said it was because Kartik was fat. Can you imagine someone saying that? I mean, I have been fat for most of my life, but that doesn't mean that is the only thing you can see in a person. There is so much more than just physical appearance.

- Another reason I agreed to marry Kartik was that my father was introducing me to men who were about ten years older than me. That was insane, like marrying my older sister. Our thoughts wouldn't match at all. I wanted to marry someone around my age so we could talk freely and not be judged. But clearly, that didn't turn out well," she said, rolling her eyes.

8. Did you tell your siblings about your situation in the marriage? I know you have an elder sister that you could have asked for help.

- Well, I did think about it said Ira. Primarily, I told my younger brother first to gauge his reaction and as a trial to judge how Meera would act. Clearly, that was a mistake. When she told him, all he could say was, "Oh, so sex is not happening. Maybe you should go to a sexologist." She laughed at how clueless men can be about such situations.

- She was so sure she wouldn't be able to verbally explain everything to my sister, as Ira was emotionally abused by my husband. With tears in her eyes, she wrote a long text message to her elder sister, Meera, and hit send without re-reading it.

- She confronted Kartik over a call and asked him to behave properly before I even reached home. Kartik was furious and started yelling at me, saying, "This is our life. How dare you talk about it to your sister?" At that point, Ira had a throbbing ache, and confronted him with all the questions that had been in my mind for a long time. I asked him if he was stuck on his last girlfriend, if he had an affair, if he wanted an open marriage, or if he was gay. She just wanted to clear the air so I could either leave or start living her life with peace of mind. But Kartik said nothing, nothing at all. That was the cherry on top of the worst pandemic ever.

9. Why did you renew your visa in November 2020 when you had planned to leave him?

- That's something my parents didn't understand. First of all, it wasn't my idea to renew it. I had spoken to my elder sister, Meera, and she insisted I renew my visa. My visa was set to expire in December 2020, and with no end to the pandemic in sight, I couldn't live there illegally. So, I had to renew it or travel back to India. Travelling wasn't an option since flights weren't operating, so I had to renew my visa. Kartik got some papers from his company stating that I was his wife, along with our marriage certificate. That's how I renewed my visa, as there was no other option.

10 This is the last and most important question: Did he call you since you returned? Or did he contact you in any way to say he doesn't want a divorce and wishes to give the marriage another try?

Hearing these questions, Ira gave a small laugh, as if the lawyer were telling her a joke. Mrs Gupta quickly picked up on the cue that he had done nothing of the sort. Ira's amusement was tinged with pain, not in tears but in the silence that followed, before she continued with the last part of her story.

Ira explained that since Mr Narendra Modi had started the Vande Bharat flights to bring people back to India, she had faced significant financial loss, including twice having her flights cancelled and incurring additional costs for COVID tests. When she asked Kartik to help her get a refund from Vistara Airlines after another flight cancellation, he dismissively said it was no big deal to lose some money and she could try again tomorrow. This infuriated Ira, especially since just a few days earlier, Kartik had asked her for money because he was struggling to pay rent. Now, he was being so irresponsible.

He had once said that marriage was a partnership between two people, implying that if she wasn't working, her father should provide for her share. When Ira offered the money, she had earned while working in India, Kartik slyly remarked, "That's our backup plan. Why don't you ask your father? He's rich, right? He can give you the money." This infuriated her. Ira retorted that it was a pandemic, people were losing jobs, and hiring was scarce—how was she supposed to find a job? If marriage was truly a partnership, then why didn't he pay for any of the wedding functions and instead forced her father to cover all the expenses for the engagement, haldi (ceremony of applying turmeric), and the grand wedding? Kartik had no answer for that, and now he seemed okay with losing money.

Eventually, she secured a seat on an Air India flight via Vande Bharat and paid another 120 pounds for a COVID test. She informed Kartik about her flight, but he was so disinterested that he forgot and was surprised when Ira woke him up in the middle of the night to book a cab. He did so without realizing her flight was imminent. That was the first time he had hugged her since their marriage, which had been one year and 20 days ago. With a grin, she recalled this moment.

"To cut the story short, he didn't call me when I landed. He texted me. He didn't call me when I spoke to his parents about the divorce. He didn't call me when his father said, 'Kartik is ready to accept you.' Nor did he call to say, 'I'm sorry.' And I don't expect him to call me either, if that answers your question."

There was silence in the cabin as her lawyer wrote down notes. The lawyer had a few more questions, but thankfully, her father entered the cabin, providing her a much-needed sigh of relief. Her father asked a few questions of his own while Ira sat quietly. It had been a hard, emotional day. As they were leaving the office, Mrs Gupta pulled Ira aside and asked, "Did you have any sexual relations in the past year? Did he at least try?" Ira laughed out loud and replied, "Are you kidding me? After all those answers, couldn't you guess that the answer is a resounding NO?" Then she left.

Dates Over Friends

Ira knew the divorce process would be lengthy. Mrs Gupta had already informed her that since she renewed her visa in November 2020, stating she was happily married in the UK, she couldn't challenge this status for another six months. After that, it would take at least another six months for the case in India to proceed, even with mutual consent, due to the mandatory counselling and other procedures.

Ira realized she needed to find a job to regain control of her life and achieve physical, emotional, and mental stability. She knew her parents well enough to anticipate how they would behave if she remained idle. Determined, she began applying for jobs, deciding to accept the first offer she received out of desperation. Until then, she had to endure her parents' constant criticism without complaint. They didn't inquire about what had happened to her but had plenty to say. They forbade her from discussing the divorce with anyone, including neighbours, relatives, and friends, to protect their reputation. They also didn't believe Ira and Kartik had been living in separate rooms.

Her father dismissed her claims, suggesting that no one would believe her and accusing her of being short-tempered and rude. He invalidated her experiences as unacceptable to society. Her parents insisted on maintaining appearances, telling everyone she was merely visiting to spend time with family. Ira refused to lie and urged her parents to support her despite societal pressure. She concluded that Indian parents aren't wired that way, and she chose to remain silent and aloof rather than lie, which angered her parents. However, her mental stability was more important to her than others' opinions.

Fortunately, Ira had a close-knit group of friends who understood her situation and supported her in every possible way. They met her for coffee dates, took her out for dinners and movies, and allowed her to speak freely about her struggles with the divorce, her in-laws, and her parents. She particularly remembered Avni and her husband, Namish, who had supported her during crises. When Kartik pressured her for money, demanding her father pay the rent while he spent extravagantly on dining out and online shopping, Namish offered financial help without hesitation. His words gave Ira the strength to face her hardships, although she never took his money. Namish also provided valuable advice from a man's perspective, proving to be a great support. Ira felt blessed to have such amazing friends like Avni and Namish in her life.

After months of job applications, Ira finally secured a position in medical coding and as a call representative for US healthcare in the optometry department. She aced all the interview rounds and even impressed a US-based doctor, who promptly extended an offer letter. Though the pay wasn't great and the job required night shifts, Ira, driven by desperation, decided to accept it. Her parents were against the idea, but she didn't care. Everyone around her was more concerned about societal norms than her well-being, so she took matters into her own hands.

Her job required her to work from 7 PM to 4 AM, and the office was almost 12 kilometres from her home. Initially, working the night shift was challenging, but not as difficult as driving home at 4 AM. To ease her situation, she decided to move closer to her workplace. She found a paying guest house for girls just a lane away from her office, where she would share a room with another girl. Ira was happy with this arrangement.

One day, Ira informed her parents about her decision to move closer to work, explaining how hard it was to commute at 4 AM. Her father suggested she quit the job and stay at home, but she responded, "I will be bored and frustrated if I stay at home doing nothing. It will take at least a year to get divorced, and I can't stay in the house that long. I need to start living my life again and make some new friends."

Her parents were strongly opposed to her decision, accusing her of always making poor choices and advising her to stay put and let things happen. Ignoring their comments, Ira explained that the PG was a secure place with only girls, costing 10,000 Rs per month, including attached toilet and bathroom facilities, as well as breakfast and dinner. She kept emphasizing the benefits, making it clear that she was determined to move out. She even took her parents to see the PG, but they showed little interest.

A week later, Ira moved into her new home, ready to regain control of her life. Moving into the PG was a positive change. Her office was now just a five-minute walk away, allowing her to get home by 4:05 AM and immediately rest. Since her roommate hadn't arrived yet, she had the entire room to herself. She also left her car and two-wheeler at her parents' house, freeing herself from any burdens.

Ira quickly made new friends at the PG, where most of the residents were sweet and innocent college students. They were a bit jealous of her because she was the only one allowed to come and go as she pleased due to her work, while the others had to be back by 8 PM. Her new friends often asked her to bring back food or ice cream late at night on weekends, taking advantage of her flexible schedule.

The food provided at the PG was good, especially the dinners. Ira often missed breakfast because she slept until 10 AM after finishing her shift at 4 AM, but this didn't bother her. Gradually, she began to heal, feeling more like her old self with each passing day. The supportive environment and new friendships helped her start to reclaim her life and sense of self.

Ira's new office was small, with only five people working on-site while the rest worked from home. She quickly became comfortable with her co-workers and the office owner. They often went out for movies and dinner on weekends, and breakfast on weekdays. After work, which ended at 4 AM, they would play badminton together. Working the night shift turned out to be enjoyable for Ira, freeing her from negative thoughts.

However, her dose of negativity often resurfaced when she visited her parents' house. Her father insisted she take her car to have more freedom after work. She refused several times before eventually giving in. Despite this, she was determined not to lose her newfound sense of freedom. Her parents clung to the idea that the job wasn't suitable for her and that she shouldn't be living in a PG. While Ira briefly considered their perspective, she ultimately decided that as long as she was happy and content, it was the right choice for her.

Her friends encouraged her to start dating again, not necessarily to find a boyfriend but to meet new people and broaden her horizons. They even downloaded a dating app on her phone, set up her profile, and right-swiped on men they thought matched her taste. This changed the game for her. Now, every other Sunday, she went out to meet new people with an open mind, even though she knew she wasn't ready for a serious relationship yet. Meeting new people lifted her spirits, especially when her friends were busy with their own lives.

Ira stopped sharing her past with new acquaintances, realizing it often made her sad. By keeping her past to herself, she found it easier to open up to new experiences and start to spread her wings.

Certainly! Here is a revised version of the text:

There was no escaping her parents, whose constant scrutiny often left her doubting herself. It had been less than two months since her visit to the lawyer, yet here she was again, as if she had never left. She kept urging Ira's father to speak with her in-laws, but he was too irritated to engage, especially since her father-in-law incessantly talked and falsely accused Ira of new transgressions. The reality was quite different from the narrative Kartik presented.

Once, her father-in-law told Ira, "You drank a whole bottle of wine and kept vomiting, yet he never complained. He supported you through your drinking problems, and this is how you repay him?" In reality, Ira explained, "I told him I wasn't a fan of wine, but your so-called 'son' insisted it was an expensive bottle I should drink. When I refused, he forced it down my throat, so of course, I vomited. Don't you dare accuse me of having drinking problems," she said firmly.

Instead of understanding the situation, her father kept complaining that her rudeness and arrogance were the source of her major problems. Ira knew her in-laws wouldn't stop their blame game and realized she needed to take action to put an end to it.

Every week days when she worked night shifts and stayed in the PG, were the best days of her life. However, weekends were a disaster as she had to visit her house and endure her parents' constant criticism about how she had wasted her life and had nothing worth living for. None of her siblings supported her, but she didn't care because she knew they never would. She thought, "If my own parents don't understand me, how could anyone else in the family?" When society claims that rich people don't have problems, they are clueless. They should be a fly on the wall at my house to understand how complicated problems can be. Middle-class people seem far more understanding than the wealthy. The rich lack the basic decency to consider that their words might hurt someone; they walk all over others' feelings without caring or apologizing. When her father-in-law called her again, Ira had had enough. He said, "Kartik asked you to visit a counsellor. Why didn't you agree? Are you having an affair?"

Furious, Ira resolved to be straightforward. "You don't know a thing about your son," she replied. "He had a word with Meera and couldn't listen to her either, and you're talking about counselling? Let's get a medical report to see if your son is fit to be married or even have sex." Her father-in-law fell silent. Ira continued, "I have a better idea: let's present that report to a court. And why are you saying all these things when your son hasn't even bothered to call me once? Does that mean something is wrong with him? Don't you dare call me again unless you have proof." She then disconnected the call.

She knew she had crossed a line with her in-laws, but it was necessary to get things back on track. Now, she needed to change the lawyer and convince her dad to do so, which she knew would be a difficult task. However, she couldn't back out now. She spent a week making detailed notes on what she needed to say and how to handle any potential questions or anger from her father. When she felt ready, she went back home and told her dad that she had something important to discuss, asking him to let her speak without interruption before he responded. Surprisingly, he agreed.

"Papa," she began, "the lawyer you selected isn't working out. She's not doing anything and always expects you to handle everything. You know how my father-in-law is; he doesn't let anyone talk. He doesn't even pause to breathe," she said with a grin, noticing a small smile on her dad's face. "Don't you think we need a lawyer who can speak his language and get things done without our constant involvement? This isn't our area of expertise, and no matter what we say, things are getting worse. If I'm going to get out of this without losing my sanity, we need a strong lawyer, and Mrs Gupta isn't it. I understand she's Meera's relative, but why should I suffer because of her? I'll apologize to her, but we need a new lawyer."

Her father took a couple of minutes to respond. When he finally spoke, he said, "You're right. I've been thinking the same thing." Ira was shocked. He continued, "One of my friend's sons is a lawyer in Pune. Let's go meet him."

Overjoyed, Ira exclaimed, "YESSS!" as if she had already been granted a divorce. They met Mr Abhishek Dolifude, who turned out to be the best lawyer Ira could have hoped for. He listened to her case, called her father-in-law directly, and understood that it would be a tough case. But he was not afraid of challenges. He reassured

Ira that she would soon be out of this mess and that her father didn't need to worry.

After a long, mentally exhausting day, Ira decided to go on a date to meet someone new and enjoy a good evening. She was planning to meet a guy named Jaydeep, known as JD, so she texted him to catch up for a drink. JD suggested a place called Talli and was eager to meet. When Ira saw JD for the first time, she was shocked. He didn't look like his picture on the dating app, but she had swiped right because his dimples were cute. They had a great conversation. Ira had just one bottle of beer since she wasn't keen on drinking, but JD had quite the capacity, downing almost eight pegs of Jack Daniels neat with just ice. When it was time to leave, Ira offered to drop him off, but JD insisted on dropping her at her PG. It was funny because she had her car and it was only a 10-minute drive. Still, JD dropped her off and then booked a cab for himself.

Later that night, back in her room, Ira couldn't stop smiling. JD wasn't just charming because of his dimples but also because of how he treated her. He came all the way to drop her off, something she had never experienced before. JD texted her after reaching home, saying he enjoyed her company, which made her very happy. Lying in bed, she thought, "Maybe it was just a good day." A good lawyer and a good friend, all in one day—she felt lucky as she drifted off to sleep, still in her clothes, a bit tipsy and overflowing with happiness.

Ira had been feeling lonely as most of her friends were married and busy with their lives. She joined several dating and matrimony apps to find someone to date, not necessarily to marry. She talked to four or five people every day to stay busy and maintain a social life. Some turned into good friends, but she hadn't found someone she could enjoy dating. Despite the exhaustion of constantly meeting new people and reliving her failed marriage, she persevered, telling herself in the mirror that she had to keep trying. Her life oscillated between "I hate men" and "I love men."

Living in a paying guest (PG) accommodation with about 50 other girls, Ira had an interesting life. The girls often complained about the food, and stealing each other's clothes and food was common. Ira made friends with five or six mature girls on the ground floor and stayed out of the food protests, which made her unpopular with the others. She had bigger problems and was just grateful for any food. Often missing breakfast, she ordered lunch and shared it with the warden, Nikita, who became a good friend. Initially, Nikita was hesitant to share food, fearing Ira would ask for money, but Ira's genuine offer led to their friendship. They bonded over shared meals, understanding that food was their love language.

In 2021, during the pandemic, most girls left the PG to return home, leaving only a few behind, including Ira and Nikita. Ira, working in healthcare, had to go to the office. One day, she saw a girl crying, missing her family and friends. Ira got special permission from Nikita to take the girls out for ice cream and a drive, promising to bring them back by midnight. She proposed the idea to the remaining girls, who were excited and happy. On a Sunday evening, Ira cancelled her date to take the girls out. They enjoyed ice cream, took pictures, laughed, and felt the cool breeze during the drive. It was one of the best days Ira had ever had, filled with true happiness.

14TH February 2022

Today marks the anniversary of my freedom from my ex-husband. It's been a year since I returned to India to quarantine, and I've decided to celebrate this milestone with one of my dearest friends, Krupa. Krupa and I met at university in London. Though we were enrolled in different courses, we quickly became great friends, fantastic flatmates, and incredible partners, despite having vastly different personalities.

Some people leave an indelible mark on your life, and Krupa is one of them. When I first saw her at the international student centre, I never imagined we'd become friends. She was surrounded by a group of guys, laughing and flirting, earning the nickname "Crisps." I turned to my friend Kovisha from Mauritius and, with a raised eyebrow, asked, "Crisps like chips? What's her real name?" Just then, another girl joined our conversation, introducing herself as Juhi with a witty smile. My immediate response, along with Kovisha's, was, "You mean Juhi Chawla?"—A nod to the famous Bollywood actress. Juhi confirmed, and that's how our friendship began.

Juhi then introduced us to Krupa. We chatted briefly before heading off for coffee and cookies. The international community centre at Greenwich University's Pembroke building was a weekly gathering spot for international students. We'd sit, talk, share snacks, and make friends. Attending these gatherings became a ritual, especially cherished during London's cold and rainy weather. The more I talked with Krupa, the more I realized she was like any other girl, though she craved attention from the opposite gender. Her bold clothing choices, which I would never consider wearing, often made her the centre of attention—a fact that never bothered me, but Juhi had her insecurities and would often criticize Krupa's appearance. I, however, believed in respecting boundaries and only offered my opinion when asked.

Eventually, I needed to move out of my university housing. Initially, I planned to find an apartment with Kovisha, but our budget preferences didn't align. I wanted an affordable place close to the university to save on commute costs. I found a house with five rooms: one occupied by an Italian couple on the ground floor, a large room on the second floor shared by several people, and three vacant rooms on the third floor with a shared bathroom. Living alone on the third floor seemed risky, so I invited Krupa to take one of the rooms and suggested we find another girl for the third room, ensuring it would be an all-girls floor. Krupa agreed, and that's how our incredible journey of friendship began.

We shared late-night talks, took late-night walks, and worked on our projects together. Our days started with breakfast and tea on the balcony, under the jealous gaze of our friend Juhi from her balcony. We balanced part-time jobs, university, and silly games in the garden across our house. Each day felt like it should never end, which is why I decided to celebrate this Valentine's Day with Krupa. To relive old memories and create new ones, I decided to travel to Bangalore, where Krupa now lives.

Ira travelled to Bangalore on Monday. Krupa had told her she would pick her up from the airport, as they had planned to stay together in a hotel and have a fun party. After exiting the airport, Ira was looking for Krupa when a text message popped up on her phone: "Come to the parking lot." Ira thought, "Oh cool, she got her new car," since Krupa couldn't stop talking about it. But to Ira's shock, there was Krupa on a yellow moped, wearing a matching yellow helmet and smiling sheepishly.

Dragging her bag, Ira started yelling, "How could you bring a moped to pick me up? Where am I going to put my bag? Can this bike even handle both of us?" Krupa laughed like she had cracked a joke. She explained that it was Monday and Bangalore was packed with traffic. Ira thought for a moment; she had only travelled to Bangalore on weekends before because it was more convenient. Now, since she was between jobs, she could travel on a weekday.

With a grin, Ira placed her bag at the front of the moped and hopped on behind Krupa. As they rode off, she asked, "Why yellow?" Krupa smiled and said, "You'll see," with a grin. As Krupa navigated the chaotic Bangalore traffic on her moped, weaving through cars and cabs like she was solving a maze, they hit a traffic jam. Ira could see it was going to be a long ride; their hotel was 14 kilometres away on MG Road, deep in the city, and the traffic was terrible. Meanwhile, Krupa, being her chatty self, struck up a conversation with a rickshaw driver, laughing and talking as if they were the only two people in the world, drawing stares from everyone around them.

Krupa asked Ira if she was dating anyone. Ira replied that she wasn't and wasn't looking to, though she was on a matrimonial site. Krupa gave her a sidelong glance but didn't press further. When Krupa asked about her sex life, Ira couldn't respond, overwhelmed by emotions. To lighten the mood, Krupa started telling a story about meeting a guy named Maan during an outing. They went for a drink, and when Maan, slightly tipsy, tried to kiss her, he ended up falling down. Krupa, rather than helping him up, just moved to another table and watched him. Ira burst out laughing and asked if Maan ever woke up or if she ended up with someone else. Krupa, grinning, admitted she called a "friend with benefits" instead, not wanting to waste a nice dress on a drunk.

Ira agreed, saying men were often disappointing and they shouldn't wait around for them. The traffic finally cleared, and they continued their journey in silence. When they reached the hotel, Krupa pointed out that the moped had saved them at least an hour in the heavy traffic.

After checking into their room, they lay on the bed, and Krupa asked Ira to share a similar story. Ira smiled and said her story was worse, having wasted both her night and her dress. She began, "I travelled to Mumbai for an international food conference and stayed at the Novotel with a great discount. I had been chatting with this guy named Ashish for two months. He had a PhD from Stanford and a stable job. He insisted we meet in the hotel lounge, which I found odd since I wanted to explore Mumbai."

"Anyway, we agreed to meet at 8 PM. He was late and unreachable, and I decided I'd wait only 15 more minutes before calling my friends to go out. He finally showed up with a bunch of excuses. He ordered wine while I had a hot toddy because of a cough. I thought it was childish for a guy to drink wine. We talked for a while, and when he got tipsy, I suggested we leave because I was sleepy. He suggested we sleep in my room. Thinking he was joking, I played along, but he was serious."

"After paying the bill, half of which I covered, he followed me to the lift, insisting he come to my room. I firmly told him no, and he drunkenly claimed he had money and often stayed in five-star hotels. He then stumbled to the reception, pretending he'd booked a room, but returned saying it was too expensive. I knew he was faking it to get laid. He sat there, claiming he'd wait until he sobered up to leave. I wished him good night, but as I was about to leave, he grabbed my hand, saying I should feel bad and take him to my room."

"I laughed in his face, telling him that education didn't change how men behaved. I told him if he couldn't handle his drinks, he should stick to mocktails. I wasn't the kind of girl to fall for such tricks and could find better company if I wanted a fling. I wished him good night and left."

Both women laughed heartily at Ira's story, feeling a shared sense of camaraderie and empowerment. They shared a few more stories about their lives while lying on the bed. When Krupa checked the time, she exclaimed, “Come on, let’s get ready!” It was already 7 PM. Ira rolled out of bed, opened her bag, and started changing. Meanwhile, Krupa, with her usual unique fashion sense, put on an outfit that made Ira ask, “Are you sure you want to wear that if we’re planning to ride the moped?” Krupa replied sternly, “NO, I’ve got my car, which is how we’re going.” Ira sighed in relief.

Soon we were out in Bangalore traffic, well-dressed and ready to have a blast. The best part was that Ira didn’t need Zomato or Google to find a place; Krupa had already planned everything. She took Ira to the rooftop restaurant called Kaze Bar & Kitchen. It was the most beautiful restaurant, with a sophisticated and chic ambience that combined modern elegance with a touch of urban flair. Located on the rooftop, it offered stunning panoramic views of the cityscape, making it perfect for both day and night visits. The restaurant had a lively and vibrant energy, making it an ideal spot for romantic dinners. Krupa had booked a table for two.

We had a few drinks—well, I had a few since Krupa was driving and only had a beer. We reminisced about our university days, part-time jobs, and late-night adventures, sharing fun and laughter from years ago. We missed Juhi, too, as she used to live in Bangalore, and we had great fun with her during past visits.

After drinks and a bit of food, we left for a long drive. Krupa spoke about my wedding and how she enjoyed it with Suzan, who came to Pune, India, from Cairo, Egypt, with her mom. Suzan Ali, my classmate for a Master's in Biotechnology at Greenwich University, often visited our house, and that's how we three became close-knit friends. "Good old days with good old memories," Ira said at the end.

We were on Airport Road at 2 AM when Krupa suddenly used the handbrake, jolting Ira as the car came to a halt. Puzzled, Ira looked at her, and Krupa screamed, "Let's eat ice cream!" Ira, slightly drunk, said, "Don't scream, Krupa, I can hear you." Krupa turned the car around like in Tokyo Drift and raced toward an ice cream shop. Silently, Ira said, "It's almost 3 AM. Where do you think we will get ice cream?" "Baskin Robbins," Krupa replied slyly.

They parked the car in the middle of nowhere, and Krupa decided to get a 250 ml tub of Bavarian Chocolate. She told the shopkeeper, "That's for my girlfriend; it's Valentine's Day, after all." He looked shocked, thinking they were a couple, but Ira played along, spanked Krupa, and said, "Thank you, dear, I love you," as they left the shop.

Back in the car, Ira opened the tub of Bavarian Chocolate, her favourite flavour, and fed a spoonful to Krupa while she drove. They ate the ice cream in silence, with Krupa glancing at Ira every now and then. When they reached the hotel at around 4:30 AM, Ira asked, "Krupa, are you okay? Why are you looking at me like that?"

Krupa replied, "Don't you know? Get out of the car and you'll realize."

Ira got out, still puzzled. Krupa pulled her to the reception area, where there was a huge mirror. "Look," Krupa said. Ira glanced at the mirror and burst out laughing. The ice cream she thought she was eating had fallen all over her dress. Her Chinoise Green dress had turned brown with Bavarian Chocolate, and she hadn't noticed at all.

Krupa joined in the laughter, and they giggled for a few minutes before heading to their room. Krupa helped Ira change, and they both jumped on the bed, falling asleep with hearts full of love and laughter.

The next day, February 15th, Ira had a flight back to Pune at 2 PM. They woke up at 9 AM, and Krupa decided to skip breakfast and go straight for lunch. Ira argued, insisting they go for breakfast since she needed to reach the airport by 12 PM. However, Krupa, being her stubborn self, had other plans. They got ready and left the hotel for an early lunch or brunch at another restaurant called 13th Floor.

To Ira's surprised Krupa had already placed the order. They were greeted with two glasses of white wine, and they toasted to their friendship. Then, the meal arrived: two plates of butter garlic lobster, served whole with the meat cooked to perfection in butter and garlic. Ira was in awe but kept glancing at her watch, worried about missing her flight. Despite the time crunch, they devoured the delicious lobster, savouring every bite along with the wine.

By 12:30 PM, Ira made the payment and urged Krupa to race against time to drop her off at the airport. Krupa drove swiftly, and they arrived at 1:45 PM. Ira sprinted through the airport as if her life depended on catching this flight, likening it to a dramatic scene from a Shahrukh Khan movie where the hero runs to his lover. Thankfully, she made it just in time, with her bag in tow.

Once settled on the flight, Ira texted Krupa, thanking her for the incredible day and the wonderful memories that would last a lifetime.

Back to pavilion

Ira looked forward to transitioning from being a paying guest to renting an apartment in Viman Nagar. With a new job and a day shift for a change, she anticipated nights filled with personal time and enjoyment. Early in the morning, she began packing, surprised at how much she had accumulated in her small cupboard. By the time she was done, she had one large bag and one small bag. Suddenly, the reality of saying goodbye to the wonderful girls she had lived with and the cherished experiences they shared hit her.

Arriving at her new apartment, Ira placed her bags down and sat on the sofa, contemplating her future. The space was silent and calm, just what she needed. She closed her eyes, seeking peace but feeling a bit scared, knowing things could go wrong. Standing in front of the mirror, she gave herself a pep talk, "I will be faithful to my work, and these will be the best days of my life. I will be happy and fulfilled, and I won't let anything go wrong." She took a deep breath and exhaled slowly.

Unpacking didn't take long. Excited, she danced to music, smiling all the while. Her new one-bedroom apartment on the fourth floor was fully furnished. The small balcony was too narrow to sit on, so she simply stood there, gazing at the sky. She quickly made a list of things she needed to buy. Around 7 in the evening, she went out to get new curtains, an electric stove for making omelettes and coffee, and some groceries. She also picked up dinner on her way back. Settling into her own place felt like living in a cozy cocoon. After dinner, she went to bed early, ready for her first day at work.

The next morning, Ira woke up early, swept the house, made a cup of coffee, and soon got ready for her new job at HCL Solutions as a Medical Coder and AR Caller. Although she lacked experience as an AR Caller (Account Receivables), she wasn't afraid of challenges. She knew a good pep talk would help her soar. The first day at work wasn't hectic—just introductions and a few coding tasks. Mr Harinder Singh, who had hired her, seemed pleased to see her working. She considered him a colleague at first.

As the days passed, Ira noticed Mr Singh's flirtatious behaviour towards all the female employees. She thought to herself that a bit of harmless flirting was okay, given he was maybe fifty years old. However, it wasn't her place to say anything. But soon, Mr Singh started cornering her, inviting her for coffee and dinner dates, which she respectfully declined. Given that he was the company owner, Ira couldn't afford to lose her job. She finally agreed to a coffee date, thinking it wouldn't do any harm. To her dismay, Mr Singh shamelessly proposed being her "sugar daddy," promising better pay and position if she agreed. She took it as a joke and changed the topic.

A few days later, Mr Singh asked her out for dinner. Ira knew it was a trap but felt confident she could handle it. She agreed, selecting the restaurant with a cunning smile. That evening, she informed her team members about Mr Singh's plan and invited them all for dinner, scheduling their arrival at 8:30 PM while she met Mr Singh at 8 PM. When her team members arrived, Mr Singh was in shock, his eyes burning with anger. Ira didn't even look at him again. She chatted and laughed with her team, enjoying the moment of triumph. She had turned the tables, outsmarting Mr Singh and leaving him speechless. This marked the beginning of Ira's new life in Viman Nagar—one filled with challenges but also opportunities for personal growth and victory. She knew that one day Mr Singh would come after her if she outsmarted him. So, she began to avoid him and focused more on her work. There was something off about this place, though. She couldn't quite put her finger on it. Perhaps it was the male-dominated environment. She was the only woman on a team of 20, and there were very few women in other teams as well. Maybe Mr Singh's behavior was driving everyone away. Her days were a cycle of work and home, with brief tea breaks with friends at a small joint where they could get snacks and coffee while others smoked and shared office gossip. Trying to be healthier, Ira had cut down on coffee, opting for lemonade or black tea, and joined a mess for lunch and dinner, hoping the simple meals would help her feel better.

Her parents, however, were still unhappy with her life choices. They didn't care when she told them she had rented an apartment in Viman Nagar, close to her workplace. She thought they would be pleased she was moving from a paying guest arrangement to her own place, but they remained discontent.

Despite her parents' disapproval, Ira began enjoying her independence and started dating again, meeting new people from dating apps. On weekends, she preferred staying at her place over visiting her parents, finding peace in solitude. She would clean her house, play music, dance, and then collapse on her bed, staring at the ceiling. The silent house she had longed for now felt uneasy, but she dismissed it as fatigue from household chores.

One afternoon, she fell ill with a severe headache and vomiting. She realized it might be the lemonade she drank near her office, suspecting it was made with bad water. Drained of energy, she called her friend Priya from work, who brought her medicine, but nothing helped. She missed work for a couple of days and emailed Mr Singh, but he didn't reply. Ira feared he would seek revenge.

When Priya suggested calling her parents, Ira refused vehemently. Even if she were dying, she wouldn't call them. Priya, shocked, continued to help Ira. On the third day, Priya spoke to Mr Singh about Ira's condition. After work, Priya found Ira fainted in the kitchen, helped her to bed, gave her electrolytes, and insisted on calling her dad. Ira resisted, but Priya called her dad and handed

Ira the phone. Her dad told her to take a cab home, so Priya helped Ira pack and booked a cab.

At home, her mother made a snide remark, and her father, slightly more compassionate, let her rest. After a week, Ira returned to work only to be fired by Mr Singh for inconsistency and failing to inform her team. Despite showing emails as proof, Mr Singh was unyielding. There was no HR to appeal to, as he had driven them away too. Insulted, Ira packed her things and left.

Back home, Ira was angry, not because she lost her job, but because she needed to find a new one within a month to avoid returning to her parents' home. The following evening, she called her dad to inform him about her job loss and assured him she would find a new one within a week. Her dad, surprisingly delighted, suggested she come home, implying she didn't need to work and could just stay at home. This comment infuriated her, but she held back her anger and ended the call with a curt, "OK."

Ira took the evening off to calm herself down before starting her job search. By the end of the day, she made a detailed list outlining her job search strategy. Early the next morning, she cleaned her house, got ready, and left for a nearby coffee shop. She ordered a strong cup of coffee, opened her laptop, and began applying for jobs and scheduling interviews.

Ira had been working in the field of medical coding for almost two years, but she wasn't a certified coder. This lack of certification made it challenging to secure a job despite her experience. She had attempted the CPC (Certified Professional Coder) exam but failed on her first try. The CPC exam is a six-hour long test with 150 questions and multiple-choice questions. It is an open-book exam. Despite being open-book, it is quite difficult, involving massive books similar to those used in medical school. These books contain alphanumeric codes for every drug, disease, operation, medical procedure, and more. The process involves converting all patient interactions into codes and submitting the CMS 1500 claim form to insurance companies to get payments for the hospital services provided.

Passing the CPC exam requires a minimum of 70%, and Ira had scored 68% on her first attempt after a year of experience. This was disheartening, but she knew nothing had ever come easily to her. She considered retaking the exam but decided to postpone it.

As the month drew to a close, she still hadn't secured a job, and her finances were becoming increasingly strained. With no other options, she reluctantly packed her things and moved back in with her parents. The prospect was daunting, but she had no choice.

Gone are the days like winds that blew,
Over and over again like cycles anew.
Ends that brought chaos, made everything askew,
Calm and silence reigned when peace grew.

Slowly and steadily, it all declined,
I walked in clouds, as high as I could climb.
But my destiny pulled me down, time after time,
Yet I will rise again, stronger, in my prime.
I will fly again, my spirit won't wane,
My wings are strong, to soar high once again.

The daunting memories

Ira hadn't written anything for years. She loved to read fiction and write poetry when overwhelmed with emotions. Now, emotions surged within her, causing her hands to tremble as if she were cold. Checking her temperature, she found it was indeed cold. "What could it be?" She wondered aloud. Ira, a highly educated individual with a BSc and MSc in Biotech, along with a diploma in pharmacy and medical coding, often analysed her symptoms. She concluded she was experiencing anxiety: tremors, cold sweats, and brain fog. "Damn it," she exclaimed, realizing this was yet another challenge to face.

She drove back home, suitcases in tow, and paused outside for a moment, giving herself a pep talk: "We're back to square one, but we'll handle it wisely. We don't care what people or parents say. We can do this." She stepped inside, greeted her mom who was cooking, and headed to her room as if nothing had changed. Her mom, sensing the tension, responded sarcastically, "Good you're here." Ira, known for her own sharp wit, felt a pang of fear—was she becoming like her mother, whom she disliked?

When her dad returned from work, he smiled warmly at Ira and said, "It's good to have you back home. Feels like my tea buddy is back." Ira returned his smile, but it felt empty.

Ira knew she needed to find a job—and fast—if she wanted to be free and fly again. But she also knew it was going to be hard. She wondered why she had said yes to working with Mr Singh when she knew it wouldn't last long. The answer was clear: a night shift converted to a morning shift, good pay, and a move to a nicer part of the city—all these perks had lured her into working with that jerk of a person. Well, what's done is done, she thought. Time lost is time that won't come back.

Determined to move forward, Ira opened her laptop and started her job search. Days passed, but she wasn't able to secure even an interview, leaving her heartbroken. One afternoon, she heard her phone ringing from the living room. "Why is my phone in the living room? Am I so engrossed that I don't know what is going on in the outside world?" She wondered, pulling herself out of her room and running to pick up the call in the hope it was a job interview.

But to her disappointment, it was Shanti calling—Shanti, as in Tushar, her ex-boyfriend. She stared at the phone until the call disconnected. "Why the hell is he calling now? What does he want?" She thought. It had been more than two years since they last had any contact. Old memories flooded back, and she was transported to the Starbucks in Aundh, Pune, where she had last met him.

It was the day she had finally decided to say yes to his proposal. She remembered visiting the salon, washing her hair, and wearing his favourite grey and orange sweatshirt. She was ready to answer "yes" to his question: "Would you marry me?" She had taken a month to decide, even though everyone knew her answer was always going to be yes.

When Tushar arrived at the coffee shop, he sarcastically complimented her appearance. Unable to contain her excitement, Ira blurted out, "My answer is yes! I spoke with my sister, and my brother knows you. My sister will convince my parents. Yes, yes, yes, I am ready to marry you."

But instead of joy, she saw sadness in his eyes. "I am sorry, Ira," he said. "My mom doesn't like you. She's already found a girl for me, and I can't say no to her. You were late to say yes, and now there's nothing I can do."

Ira was numb. She tried to speak, but no words came out. She wiped her tears and said, "But you proposed to me. And now you're marrying someone else? Are you serious? Can't you talk to your parents?" After a few minutes of silence, Tushar simply said, "Okay," and left, spilling his coffee in the process.

They hadn't spoken since, and two months later, she learned from a friend that Tushar had gotten married. When she arrived late to a reunion party, her friend Rutu pulled her aside to break the news. Despite the shock, Ira decided she wouldn't leave the party. She dressed up, put on a brave face, and decided to confront Tushar.

At the party, Ira acted nonchalant. She greeted Tushar and met his new wife, Priyanka, with feigned enthusiasm. "Congratulations! He's going to be the best husband ever," she said with a smirk. Tushar was visibly uncomfortable as Ira laughed, drank, and danced with her friends.

The party was in full swing. Laughter and chatter filled the room, creating a lively backdrop for Ira's internal turmoil. She had decided she wouldn't let Tushar's presence ruin her evening. Instead, she chose to enjoy herself, mingling with friends and pretending not to care about the newlyweds.

As the night wore on, Ira found herself at the bar, ordering her favourite drink—Jack Daniel's on the rocks. She was just taking a sip when she noticed a tall, attractive man standing a few feet away, glancing in her direction. Sensing an opportunity to distract herself, she gave him a coy smile.

Ira had dressed to impress. She wore a deep V-neck green top that was sleeveless and paired it with her favourite blue jeans. It wasn't her usual style—her mother never approved of such outfits—but for her friends' parties, she made an exception. Tonight, she was determined to look her best, no matter what.

After a few drinks with her friends, Ira felt the warm, familiar buzz of Jack Daniels neat on the rocks. Rutu, her ever-loyal friend, stayed by her side, both wary and supportive. The music thumped in the background, a pulsating beat that matched her racing heart. It wasn't long before she spotted Tushar across the room, his eyes following her every move.

Deciding to be bold, Ira sauntered over to the bar. She felt the stares, the curiosity, but she didn't care. She was here to reclaim her night, her confidence, her self-worth. A handsome guy, tall with dark hair and a charming smile, sidled up next to her.

"Hey," he said, flashing a grin. "Can I buy you a drink?"

Ira smiled back, her eyes twinkling with a mix of mischief and challenge. "Sure, you can buy the next one?"

As the bartender prepared her drink, they exchanged pleasantries. His name was Arjun, and he had a warm, engaging demeanour. Ira found herself laughing at his jokes, her earlier tension melting away. She could feel Tushar's gaze burning into her back, but she ignored it, focusing instead on Arjun's easy conversation.

"So, what brings you here tonight?" Arjun asked, leaning in slightly to be heard over the music.

"Just here to catch up with some old friends," she replied, taking a sip of her drink. "And maybe make some new ones."

Arjun chuckled; his eyes sparkling. "Well, I'm glad I'm one of the new ones."

Just then, Tushar appeared beside them, his expression unreadable. Ira turned to face him, her smile never wavering.

"Tushar!" She exclaimed, her voice dripping with feigned surprise and sweetness. "I didn't expect to see you here. Have you met Arjun?"

Tushar's eyes flicked to Arjun, then back to Ira. "No, I haven't."

Arjun extended his hand, and Tushar shook it briefly, his grip firm. "Nice to meet you, man," Arjun said, oblivious to the tension.

Ira decided to up the ante. "Arjun was just telling me about this amazing new restaurant downtown. We should all go sometime."

Tushar's jaw tightened. "Maybe," he said curtly.

Ira turned her attention back to Arjun. "So, what's good there?"

Arjun launched into a description of the menu, and the different cuisines that they had; she was listening to Arjun's chat through her ears and could see Tushar's frustration growing from the corner of her eyes. After a few more minutes, Tushar couldn't take it anymore. He stepped closer, trying to interject, but Ira smoothly placed her hand on Arjun's arm, laughing at his story.

Finally, Tushar snapped. "Ira, can we talk?"

Ira raised an eyebrow. "We are talking, Tushar. But if you need something specific, I'm sure you can wait until I'm done here."

Arjun, sensing the awkwardness, offered a polite exit. "I'll get us another round," he said, giving Ira a sympathetic smile before heading to the bar.

As soon as he was out of earshot, Ira faced Tushar, her expression hardening. "What do you want, Tushar?"

"You're making a scene," he hissed.

She laughed, a bitter edge to her voice. "Oh, I'm making a scene? You should be the one leaving, not me."

Tushar glanced around, aware of the curious stares from their friends. "Can we please talk somewhere private?"

Ira crossed her arms, leaning back against the chair. "There's nothing left to talk about, Tushar. You made your choice. Now, live with it."

Tushar opened his mouth to argue, but Ira cut him off. "Go enjoy your evening with your wife, she must be waiting for you, Tushar. You shouldn't be the one messing things up so soon," she said sarcastically.

She turned her back on him, rejoining Arjun and smiling as if nothing had happened. The rest of the night, she danced and laughed, ignoring the looks Tushar threw her way. It was her way of taking control, of showing him—and herself—that she was stronger than he ever gave her credit for.

As the night wound down, Ira felt a sense of triumph. She had faced her past, and while the wounds were still fresh, she had proven to herself that she could move forward. And that was a victory worth celebrating.

Now, after so many years, he had the audacity to call her. "What the hell does he want now?" She wondered, unable to fathom the reason behind his sudden reappearance in her life.

Love and laughter that we shared,
Years and years where we both cared,
All came rushing back to me,
When I saw you with who should've been me.

All the light that once did shine,
Dimmed the path that was once mine,
With a strange smile on your face,
All our memories surfaced in a painful trace.

You left me once, you left me behind,
All those gazes that were once mine,
You gave them to her, you gave her your all,
You broke me to pieces, yet I will never fall.

Off your guilt, you'll live your life,
You'll feel it again when you see my strife,
You'll come back, crawling to me,
For it wasn't one, nor two, but nine years you'll need to repay me.

Ira ignored the call, picked up her bag, and left the house to get a good cup of coffee. By now, she was very independent and hardly required company for anything. She had trained herself to go to movies and coffee dates alone, always believing it was better to be alone than with someone who would give her a headache that would last a lifetime.

She headed to a new coffee place that had recently opened in Kothrud, Pune, called "Third Wave Coffee." One of her friends had recommended it, praising its excellent coffee and her favourite cinnamon bun. Though not particularly interested in food at the moment, what Ira really needed was a steaming cup of hot coffee to help calm her mind and provide a break from all the horrible memories flooding back.

Upon entering, she ordered a French Vanilla Latte, one of the bestsellers, and chose a table for two near the window. From there, she could observe the hustle and bustle of the street outside while enjoying the silence she longed for. Sipping her coffee and staring at the traffic, her mind wandered to places she didn't want to revisit.

It was the first day of her Math and Science class at OM Classes, where she had joined with her friend Rutu (Rutuja Khairmode, her school friend) during their 11th standard. There were about 15 students in the class, a mix of girls and boys from different colleges. Ira had chosen Abasaheb Garware College to avoid the dress code required by the college affiliated with her former school. Rutu, on the other hand, had joined the college with the dress code, and Tushar was her classmate who had also joined OM Classes.

On the first day, no one was really focused on studies; everyone was busy chatting and making new friends. Ira was arguing with Rutu about going to see "Pyar Ke Side Effects," (Side effects of love) a Bollywood movie she was eager to watch. Rutu, who hated sitting in a theatre for three long hours, was not interested. The guy sitting in front of them turned around, having overheard their conversation, and offered to go to the movie with Ira.

Both Ira and Rutu were shocked. Ira, being herself, coolly said, "Cool, we'll go today at 4 PM. Do you have a bike? If not, come to the theatre directly." Both Rutu and Tushar were taken aback by her straightforwardness. Rutu, knowing Ira inside out, reassured

Tushar, "Don't worry, she's always been like that. As long as I don't have to go with you guys, I'm okay. Thank you for that, Tushar."

Thinking about the old memories, Ira smiled to herself. But when someone collided with her table, the smile vanished, bringing her back to the present. She knew she couldn't just let that call go unanswered and needed to see why Tushar had called. She needed closure.

Ira picked up her mobile and called Tushar. As soon as he picked up, she demanded, "Why did you call me? What do you want?"

There was a moment of silence on the other end before she heard his voice. "Hello, you there?" She pressed.

"Yes, I'm here," Tushar responded. After a brief pause, he continued, "Let's catch up for old times' sake. I heard you're back from some common friends, so I thought to call you. What do you say? Can we meet up for coffee?"

She replied sharply, "Are you bringing your wife? If yes, I'll get someone too. I hate being the third wheel and I don't want you to feel uncomfortable."

Tushar, shocked and feeling guilty, said, "No, I'm coming alone. We can sit and talk."

With a noncommittal "hmmm," she cut off the call. She didn't know what she felt or why he wanted to meet her. She suspected their mutual friends had told him about her divorce, prompting his call. But she was determined not to let him gloat or make her feel bad about her hasty marriage. She knew she needed a plan before meeting him, one that would allow her to answer all his questions with confidence and integrity, showing that nothing could break her.

When she got home, she downloaded a couple of dating apps and created a profile for herself. She added just one picture of herself in a trendy outfit and another of a half-filled glass of whiskey, which she really needed. She came up with a catchy tagline: "If you like me, swipe right; if I like you, then we might catch up for a drink." The photos perfectly complemented her tagline.

She knew that on dating apps, most people judge based on looks when meeting a stranger for the first time. So, she made sure her profile picture showcased her best self. She opened the app and began swiping left and right absentmindedly. After a while, she got bored, tossed her phone aside, and went to sleep.

The next morning, she woke up with a start, as if she'd had a bad dream. She quickly searched for her phone and checked the dating app she had downloaded the night before. She had loads of messages from people who matched with her. She spent half the day chatting with them, but shared contact information with only a few. One guy, in particular, caught her attention. He was mesmerizing, with dimples that appeared when he smiled. She decided to meet him that very same day.

In the evening, she got ready for her first date, reminding herself that it was just coffee. The guy, Satyam, was tall and well-built like a hulk, which attracted Ira. They planned to meet at Starbucks on Law College Road. Ira arrived 15 minutes early, as she hated being late. To her surprise, she saw Satyam crossing the road on time, bringing a huge smile to her face. It wasn't just because he looked good in blue jeans and a crisp white shirt with folded sleeves, revealing sculpted, tattooed arms, but because he respected time as much as she did. "Oh yeah, baby, you're on time," she thought to herself. Satyam, thinking she was smiling at him, waved from afar, and she waved back.

When he arrived, he introduced himself and gave her a side hug. They sat down together. Satyam's way of talking made her laugh, though she tried to keep a straight face. His appearance was imposing, but his voice was soft and gentle, almost feminine. He shared stories about his work, and they talked about past relationships over a cup of coffee. Satyam admired how Ira had handled her life with strength, while Ira admired his success in setting up his own business at a young age.

As they said goodbye, they exchanged Instagram IDs to stay in touch. It was the best evening she had spent in a long time. However, the thought of what Tushar wanted to talk to her about still lingered in the back of her mind. She knew she had to meet him to stop the thoughts from running wild.

She picked up the phone and called Tushar. He answered on the first ring, as if he had been eagerly waiting for her call. "Hey, let's catch up for coffee at Westend," she suggested. Tushar responded with a simple "Hmm," and they confirmed the time for 7 PM on Saturday. She replied with an "OK," her tone leaving no room for argument. Despite the brief exchange, Tushar understood her completely.

Westend is a mall in Aundh, a bit far from Ira's house, but the drive would allow her some relaxing moments to herself. Driving was like therapy for her.

On Saturday, Ira arrived at the Westend mall early, around 6 PM, thinking she could do some shopping before meeting Tushar. As she stepped inside the H&M store, she heard someone call her name. She dismissed it, thinking it was her imagination. But then she heard it again. She turned around and saw Tushar, dressed in green pants and a black t-shirt, running towards her with a familiar smile. She looked at him with a grin but said nothing.

"Hi! How are you? It's been so long, two years, right?" Tushar greeted her enthusiastically. Ira glanced at her watch and replied, "We planned to meet at 7, and we will meet at 7. Right now, I'm going to do some shopping. You can go or wait till 7."

Tushar was taken aback but followed her into H&M, saying, "You can shop, and we can talk while you shop." Ira responded curtly, "I don't shop with someone else's husband. I need privacy to shop, so please leave me alone, and we shall meet at 7."

Tushar's eyes darkened with guilt. He left her alone in the store, while Ira thought, "Wow, I have a power I didn't know I had. This feels nice, and I should use it more often." Smiling, she tried on some clothes and made a few purchases.

At 7 PM, she called Tushar to ask which coffee shop they were meeting at. He told her he was waiting in the food court on the third floor. She agreed and made her way upstairs. Recognizing him from afar, she didn't smile; instead, she raised her eyebrows and walked to his table. Dropping her bags on a chair, she said, "Hi, Tushar. How are you doing? Hope you didn't get bored," he said sarcastically and sat down.

Bluntly, he replied, "No." She gave him a smile and said, "Do you want a coffee or are you just going to sit there?" He said nothing. Ira got up and said, "Okay then, seems like it's just me for coffee and maybe something to eat too." He still didn't say a word. So, she left him and got herself a cup of coffee and a glazed donut, not because she was hungry but because she really wanted a donut. She came back, sat in front of him, took a sip of coffee, and held up the donut, gesturing if he wanted a bite. Still, there was no reply.

She took a bite of the donut and closed her eyes, making an exaggerated "Hmmmm" sound. Tushar could no longer sit in silence and said, "Can you stop making those noises? Someone might think I'm doing something to you." Ira and Tushar looked at each other for a moment, burst out laughing, just like old times. For a moment, they forgot the present and were back to their good old days, laughing over double-meaning jokes.

But when Ira noticed a guy staring at her, she straightened up, stopped laughing, and took another sip of her coffee. Tushar commented, "You've become rude, and not in a good way."

Ira replied, "I'm good to people who are good to me or are friends with me. People who cheat deserve this behaviour of mine."

Tushar said nothing and started telling her about his wife, Priyanka, whom he calls Priya. He mentioned how she was similar to Ira and had a mind of her own. He explained that he had to marry Priya because his mother forced him, and what attracted him to Priya was her straightforwardness, just like Ira.

Ira's anger flared. "Stop comparing your wife to me," she yelled. "I have my own personality, and how dare you compare me with her. If you think she's like me, then why the hell did you call me here to meet you? You could have talked to your wife instead." She took a huge bite of her donut, drained her coffee in one sip, and stared at him, making it clear she wasn't interested in hearing about his wife.

Realizing his mistake, Tushar tried to explain that it wasn't his fault, but Ira dismissed his words and got up. "Please sit down, Ira. I need to talk to you," Tushar pleaded.

Ira picked up her bags and left without looking back. She was furious, and he could see it on her face. She had come to meet him, hoping for closure, but he had an agenda she wasn't aware of.

When Ira got home, she received a call from Rutu after almost five years. She was both shocked and excited to speak with her. "Hello, Ira? Is that you? Is this still your number?" Asked Rutu. Ira started laughing, "Of course, it's me. How many people did you call before asking such a silly question?" Rutu sighed in relief and joined in the laughter. They talked about how they had lost contact for over five years and how much their lives had changed. Rutu, as warm as ever, told Ira that she had made the right decision to leave her ex-husband and that she was proud of her for not suffering more than she already had.

They discussed how difficult it is for a woman to make such a decision. Rutu knew Ira well and always saw her as strong, but she never thought Ira had suffered so much in a relationship. Later, Ira mentioned that Tushar had called her. Rutu was silent for a minute before asking, "Isn't he married now? Why did he call you?" Ira replied, "How would I know? I went to meet him, and he kept telling me it wasn't his fault and that his wife is just like me." Rutu started laughing and said, "Then why did he want to meet you? He should have just talked to his wife at a coffee shop." Ira laughed and said, "I said the same thing!" They both laughed heartily.

At that moment, Ira realized that distance didn't really matter. She and Rutu were still the same and shared the same telepathy as before. They promised to stay in touch and decided to meet, even though they lived in different cities now. It would be challenging to catch up, but they both looked forward to meeting and reminiscing about old memories.

After speaking to her old friend Rutu, Ira had a huge smile on her face. Rutu was married and was expecting and the thought of her being the mom was like the best feeling ever; she knew that Rutu would be the best mom ever. She had gotten married to her college boyfriend, Sameer, and was happy. She realized that almost all of her friends were married, and most of them were either expecting or were already having babies, not that it made her sad but it was a different experience for her altogether. As now, whenever they met, they were always talking about their babies and how it kind of ruined their sexual life, so she grinned. It was just Mau (Rupali), Arohi and Jyoti who were without kid while at least Rupali and Arohi were married, Jyo was single and herself a divorced woman. Everyone was in a different phase of their life.

Stigma' Isolation

A mother-daughter relationship is one of the most unique and cherished bonds in human life. It involves nurture, respect, and, most importantly, communication. A mother is typically close to her daughter's heart, serving as a source of comfort and understanding. In an ideal relationship, there is no judgment, just a deep sense of understanding and care for each other. Honesty, trust, and a level of comfort in sharing anything without fear of being judged are what a daughter expects from her mother. Mutual respect and respecting boundaries go hand in hand, which in turn strengthens their relationship. Encouragement and support from a mother can make her daughter feel valued and close. Such a bond is marked by open communication, where both parties actively listen and support each other through life's ups and downs.

However, for Ira, this ideal was far from her reality. Her relationship with her mother was fraught with disappointment and misunderstanding. Instead of being the first person she would turn to with her troubles, Ira's mother was often the last, or not even considered at all. Ira could never understand why her mother behaved in a way that left her feeling disrespected, disgusted, and as though her boundaries were constantly being crossed.

From a young age, Ira felt overlooked by her mother. Stress eating became a problem for her early on, and instead of understanding the root of her distress, her mother would offer food as a solution and tell her to be quiet. This lack of emotional support and understanding deeply hurt Ira and fuelled a growing sense of hatred. Her mother gave all her attention to her first loving child, Meera, and always compared Ira to her or her brother. Her brother, Ishan, was the "sun" in her mother's eyes, and no matter what he did, it was always acceptable. Ira, on the other hand, felt like a sandwich stuck between the two.

As Ira entered college, the relationship worsened. Her mother judged her friends, her clothing choices, and frequently made belittling comments, as though it was her job to criticize. Achievements that should have been celebrated were ignored or met with taunts. When Ira tried to express what was bothering her, her mother would simply start yelling, making Ira feel as though everything was her fault.

Ira's father, always busy working to make ends meet, was seldom around. When he was present, he treated Meera as a worker and their son, Ishan, as a king, further spoiling him in ways the family only now began to understand. Both parents made Ira and Meera feel inferior to their brother, repeatedly emphasizing that as the boy, Ishan was the most important member of the family.

Ira recalls moments from childhood when their parents would give just one chocolate each to Ira and Meera but two to Ishan, as he was considered the "man of the house." Their parents would say things like, "This is not your house; you will soon be leaving to go to your husband's house, while Ishan will stay and take care of us." Such statements reinforced the notion that Ishan was more important simply because he was a boy.

This experience is not unique to Ira. It reflects a broader issue in many parts of Indian society, where male dominance is prevalent. Regardless of a girl's achievements, she often receives less importance compared to her male siblings, who are viewed as the center of the family's universe. This societal bias deeply troubled Ira and Meera, who, despite their frustrations, often kept silent because speaking out seemed futile. Ira felt the need for empathy, respect, and equality in familial relationships.

The actions and attitudes of Ira's parents left indelible marks on her mind and soul, creating wounds that may never fully heal. When she secured her first job, a significant milestone in her life, her parents showed no excitement or gratitude. They were indifferent to her career choice, further deepening her sense of isolation and disappointment.

One of the most painful experiences for Ira was during her divorce. At a time when she needed support the most, her parents were conspicuously absent. She vividly remembers driving to the court to sign her divorce papers and receiving a call from her father saying, "I hope you can go alone and sign the papers. If there's any problem, give me a call, but I'm sure there won't be any." His casual dismissal of the significance of the moment left her feeling utterly alone. The overwhelming emotions of guilt and sadness about her failed relationship were compounded by the absence of any family support.

Entering the court alone, while her ex-husband was accompanied by his parents, Ira felt the stark contrast of her solitude. Standing by herself with only her lawyer for support, she faced the counsellor and judge, signed the papers, and walked out alone. The emotional weight of that moment, coupled with the lack of familial presence, was something that only intensified her feelings of abandonment.

The stigma attached to her divorce was another source of pain. When Ira returned home, her parents advised her to hide her divorce from others, reinforcing the idea that she should be ashamed of her situation. They even refrained from taking her to relatives' and friends' houses for fear of what others might say. This isolation only served to alienate her further, as her parents failed to consider what she had endured in her marriage.

Their disbelief regarding her lack of a sexual relationship with her ex-husband added another layer of hurt. When her father called and instructed her to lie about the reasons for her divorce to potential suitors, it underscored their lack of trust and understanding. They expected her to conform to their narrative, regardless of her truth.

Meeting a new prospective partner brought its own set of challenges. Her parents insisted she lie about the reasons for her divorce, fearing societal judgment more than their daughter's well-being. They had the audacity to criticize her lack of confidence while simultaneously undermining her by dictating her actions and responses.

Her father's behavior was particularly contradictory and controlling. He would tell her not to be angry, yet insist she should have her own point of view. He dictated when she could express her emotions and when she needed to forgive, disregarding her feelings and autonomy. This constant control was rooted in the belief that her one wrong decision in marriage justified their continued interference and judgment.

Ira's experience raises important questions about parental responsibility and behavior. Are parents supposed to act this way? Should they prioritize societal perceptions over their child's emotional well-being? The continuous dictation of her life choices and the emotional manipulation she endured highlight a significant failure in parental support and empathy.

Ira had a great impact on her life, and so did parental actions and attitudes on a child's mental and emotional health. Her parents' lack of support, understanding, and respect left her feeling unloved and unsupported during the most crucial moments of her life. The societal stigma surrounding divorce and the gender biases within her family only exacerbated her feelings of isolation and hurt. Ira's journey underscores the need for empathy, support, and open communication in familial relationships to foster a nurturing and loving environment.

Ira's parents' decision to showcase their support by buying her an apartment seemed more about impressing others than genuinely caring for her. Her sister, Meera, had a strong influence on their parents, leading to decisions that disregarded Ira's own happiness and aspirations. Meera's belief that a high salary was essential for happiness and her insistence on Ira quitting her job demonstrated a lack of understanding of Ira's contentment with her life choices.

When Ira attempted to start her own food business, her father's initial support quickly waned under Meera's influence, forcing Ira to abandon her entrepreneurial dreams and pursue a career in IT instead. This decision was driven by a misguided belief that it would help her find a suitable husband, which Ira found frustrating and demoralizing.

Despite completing a Data Analyst course and seeking a job to regain her independence, Ira continued to face disappointment and lack of support from her family. Even when she finally secured a position as a consultant, her parents' reaction focused solely on the prospect of her finding a husband, further highlighting their lack of understanding and appreciation for her achievements.

Throughout this journey, Ira realized that her true desire was to be happy and at peace, without the societal pressures of marriage. She met people through dating and matrimony apps to appease her parents, but none of the matches resonated with her. At 35, with maturity and experience, she recognized red flags in potential partners and prioritized her own well-being over conforming to her family's expectations.

The love and support she sought in her quest,
Not found in anyone, left feeling distressed.
Yearning for respect, for emotions so pure,
What she received was the opposite, for sure.

Dismissal of dreams, a life left unmet,
Her visions shattered, with deep regret.
Empathy and care, her rightful share,
In her family's love, she hoped to find there.

Lost in attachment, to one thought she clung,
Chaos arose, her stressed soul unsung.
Each person she met brought a new pain,
Their sorrows became hers, as heavy as chain.

For the love she thought she deserved to earn,
Became a fragile dream, her heart did yearn.
Her parents perceived her lacking in might,
Courage and confidence, unseen in their sight.

To seek out love in the world's vast sea,
Required the strength they failed to see.
Her hurt remained hidden, deeply ensconced,
Her parents' neglect, a wound pronounced.

She pleaded now, "Please, no more pain,
I can't bear yours, nor handle mine's strain.
I wish to heal, to feel sunshine's glow,
To laugh again, and let self-love grow."

Her commitment now to herself proclaimed,
To find joy within, her soul reclaimed.
She must stay away from those who misread,
She needs not their doubt, but love instead.

The 2 D's - Dating ' Desire

Ira's first boyfriend was a guy named Raman who lived near her apartment. She had first noticed him in a grocery store and found him really attractive. At the time, she was in the 10th grade and often rode her bike around the neighbourhood. One day, while arguing with the shopkeeper over the wrong amount of change, she noticed Raman smiling at her, dimples appearing on both cheeks. That smile was blissful, and she knew there was a spark between them. They both felt it.

Once, while going to college, Raman followed her just to see where she went. Another time, she followed him. It felt like being in a romantic novel, experiencing a rush of desire to be with someone.

Late one night, Ira was sitting on the swing when she saw a guy waving at her from a window. Initially, she thought he was waving at someone else, so she didn't respond and continued playing by herself. She closed her eyes for a bit, and when she opened them again, she saw a shadow behind her. Startled, she turned around and there stood Raman, dressed in black trousers and a black T-shirt, smiling at her.

Ira was shocked and couldn't even stand up. She gestured for him to sit on the swing next to hers. He nodded and sat down without saying a word for some time. Finally, he broke the silence. "Ira, you need to ride your bike a bit slower. You might get hurt one day." Ira jumped off her swing, stared at him with her hands on her hips, and asked, "How do you know my name?" Raman introduced himself and explained, "My elder brother Rahul is friends with your sister. That's how I got your name," he said with a smile.

Ira, now understanding, simply said, "Oh, okay," and sat back on her swing. That was their first chat, and later they dated for like a month or so. That was her 1st boyfriend. Later in school she dated her friend Kartik Bagade; just roaming around together, they got attached to each other; not sure now if that can be called love. Ira joined Tinder and Bumble quite late after completing her Master's degree, primarily to meet new people and occasionally for a hookup. She lost her virginity relatively late as well, just before getting married. Her long-time boyfriend, Tushar, was not particularly interested in being physically intimate, and she didn't push it either.

When Ira's friend discovered she was still a virgin at the age of 30, she decided that Ira's first time should be with someone attractive and good-looking. This decision came after Tushar had married another woman. During a visit to Bangalore in September 2019 for wedding shopping with her family, Ira stayed back at a hotel with her university friends Juhi and Krupa while the rest of her family returned to Pune.

Ira had always been an old-school girl, desiring to have sex with someone she loved and intended to marry. Despite dating Tushar for nearly nine years, they never had a physical relationship. She had hoped to marry him, but that hope had faded, and she realized it was time to move on. That night, the three friends went out to party, enjoying good food and late-night drinks at BYG Brewski Brewing Company in Hennur, Bangalore.

BYG Brewski Brewing Company was their favourite spot, with its vibrant ambiance and garden-like atmosphere reminiscent of a place from the famous series *Game of Thrones*. The venue offered various cuisines and a wide range of beers, although Krupa and Ira preferred whiskey, while Juhi enjoyed beer. They arrived around 9 PM, ordered drinks and food, and reminisced about their university days, filled with laughter and games.

During the evening, a guy named Siddharth approached their table asking for a light for his cigarette, which Krupa provided. He interacted with them multiple times and eventually joined their table, along with his friend Ankit, a pilot at Air India. They exchanged life stories and continued drinking until closing time.

Juhi immediately booked a cab for them while Ankit and Siddharth stayed back, persistently inviting them to an after-party at their place. Ira, tempted by the idea of attending her first after-party, glanced at Krupa. Sensing Ira's interest, Krupa suggested, "Why not? We can join for the after-party, but I hope you have drinks and smokes." Juhi, taken aback by Krupa's suggestion, pulled her aside and said, "Are you mad? This is Bangalore. You know how people can be—they might turn out to be rapists or murderers, and it's just the three of us. What if they kidnap us?" Krupa, visibly drunk, responded with a laugh, "Oooh, I've never been kidnapped!" Juhi, however, remained adamant. "I'm going back to the hotel. I'm not interested," she insisted. Despite Ira's attempts to convince her otherwise, assuring her that they would have fun, Juhi stood firm. Eventually, Ira gave up, and they parted ways. As Juhi sat in her cab, the others bid her goodbye, leaving Ira and Krupa to join Ankit and Siddharth for the after-party.

Take 2 – Ankit was driving the car while Ira and Krupa exchanged meaningful glances, engaging in a silent conversation. Krupa broke the silence with a teasing comment, "Oh lalala... a pilot from Pune, nice choice!" Ira replied, "Oh hello! I said yes to the after-party because I've never been to one, and that's it. Besides, I don't think the pilot is interested in me, but I guess Sid is into you, so go ahead. You have my permission."

Suddenly, both burst into laughter, causing Ankit to stop the car and the boys to look at them with puzzled expressions. "What happened? Tell us too," they asked, but Krupa and Ira continued giggling like schoolgirls. Eventually, Ankit and Sid gave up, turning up the music until they reached Ankit's place.

Ankit lived in Geetanjali Society, which had several buildings. He parked the car, and they all followed him to his apartment on the fourth floor. The ride up in the elevator was silent, but as soon as they entered his apartment, Ankit turned on the music. Ira and Krupa headed to the balcony, where they could see part of the city and feel the wild wind blowing. Meanwhile, Ankit started setting up drinks and snacks, playing the host, while Sid joined the girls and asked, "I wonder what you two were laughing about in the car?"

Krupa replied, "That's for us to know and you to not," winking at Ira, who gave Sid a big smile, hinting at the joke. Suddenly, Ira's phone rang. "Who's calling you at this hour?" Krupa asked. Ira checked her phone and said, "It's Juhi."

Ira answered, "Hello, Juhi. Did you get home safely? Why are you still awake? I thought you'd be sleeping." Juhi, concerned, replied, "Ira, be safe. Don't listen to Krupa's crazy ideas. Call me anytime if you need anything."

Taking the call to another room, Ira reassured Juhi, "Juhi, I'm an adult, 30 years old. I know what's right and wrong. I can handle things, and I agree with not always listening to Krupa. I'll tell you everything when I get back. Don't worry, we'll come back when we get bored." Laughing, Juhi felt reassured and said, "Bye." Ira texted Juhi, "I love you, you're so cute," along with a thank you emoji for her concern.

Looking around the room, Ira noticed it was sparse, with just a cupboard and a washroom. She decided to wash her face but was shocked by the state of the bathroom, which reminded her of an Indian railway washroom. She abandoned the idea and headed back outside, where Krupa was calling her.

Ankit had set up a large Jenga game in the living room, and Krupa was excited. "Ira, Ankit, one team. Me and Sid, another. Let's play," she declared. Jenga is a game of physical and mental skill, involving a tower built from 54 wooden blocks. Each player takes turns removing one block from any level of the tower (except the top) and placing it on top, creating a progressively taller and more unstable structure. The game continues until the tower collapses. The player who causes the collapse loses the game. Winning requires a steady hand, strategic block removal, and careful placement.

Krupa started the game, carefully pulling a block and placing it on top. Ankit eagerly took his turn next. The game continued for about half an hour, and when it was Sid's turn, he got distracted by a phone call, causing the blocks to fall. Krupa yelled, "NOOOOOOO!" While Ankit and Ira danced around the table in a mock African tribal dance and, laughter filled all around the room.

As Sid spoke on his phone, Krupa wanted a smoke, but Ankit was out of cigarettes. He said, "Let me go out and get some. One of you can watch TV, and the other can come with me." Ira suggested Krupa go since she wanted to smoke, but Krupa, already lying on the sofa, just shook her head. Eventually, Ira had to go with Ankit. As they were leaving, Krupa pulled Ira aside and whispered, "Ja ji le apni zindagi" (Go live your life), smiling knowingly. Ira smiled back, understanding the implication.

For Ira, it was never just about having sex with someone, as she had never done it. Krupa often teased her, saying she didn't know what she was missing. Ira, being old-fashioned, believed, "How can you just have sex with someone you hardly know?" This had always been a point of contention, with Juhi and Ira on one side and Krupa on the other. Being a virgin never bothered Ira as much as it did her friends, who often laughed at her for it.

Ira opened the car window to feel the cool breeze on her face while Ankit drove. "Where will you get cigarettes at this time? It's almost 3 AM," she asked. Ankit just smiled and replied, "I know a place." Within ten minutes, he pulled into a petrol station. He advised Ira to close her window and stay in the car, and she understood, given the late hour and the safety concerns in Bangalore.

Ankit returned quickly with the cigarettes, and as they drove back, he started sharing his story. He talked about his recent divorce, becoming emotional as he spoke. Ira listened quietly, understanding he was drunk and needed to vent. He held her hand, kissed it, and asked about her ex who had cheated on her. The personal questions made Ira emotional too, though she had long moved past her ex.

Taking a longer route back, they eventually reached the society within 15 minutes. In the elevator, Ankit suddenly pushed Ira against the elevator wall, kissing her softly on her forehead and then on her lips. She was shocked but tipsy and feeling good; she kissed him back. As the elevator reached the fourth floor, before Ira could press the bell, Ankit pulled her against the inner wall, kissing her hungrily. His hands roamed, caressing her breasts and sliding under her dress to her panties. She breathed hard, his mouth on her neck, shoulders, and back on her lips, asking for more. He slid his hand into her panties, fingering her as he watched her expression of enjoyment.

Hearing someone opening the door, Ankit pulled his hand out, licked his fingers; this made her want more of him while Ankit made Ira stand in front of the door. She was in awe, thinking, "OMG, what just happened?" Staring at Ankit, she watched as he spoke to Krupa as if nothing had occurred. Krupa said, "It took you so long to come back? I was getting bored." Ankit nudged Ira, and she responded, "Oh yeah, the shop was far, and that's why it took us time to return."

Krupa and Ankit lit the cigarettes and stood on the balcony saying nothing, just lost in thoughts while Ira sat down with Sid. Sid was also from Pune, and they started a conversation in Marathi. He told her that he is married and not to tell that to Krupa while having a drink, he told her that he is having some problems with his wife and that is the reason he was staying with Ankit for some time now, though his business was in Pune. He seemed quite sober talking to her while both Krupa and Ankit were drunk. It was Ankit's idea then to watch a horror movie. While she knew that Krupa hates Horror movies, Krupa would cry and make a scene and she tried to avoid watching horror movie, but both Ankit and Sid were stubborn about watching one. They selected the movie "The Conjuring," that was the scariest movie ever for Krupa. She sat on one of the sofas with Sid close to her as if for protection from ghost while Ira sat on the other and somehow it was Ankit that held Ira as if he was scared of the ghost, which made Ira blush.

As the movie started, she could see Krupa curled up like a ball and covering her eyes with her hand and seeing the movie through her fingers, while Sid was lost in some thoughts. Ankit, on the other hand was sitting behind Ira and hugging her from behind like how those young couples sit, and that felt like trust and something that didn't feel awkward so he let him be. Then it was Sid's idea to switch off the lights for the effects that would be scarier and he even tried to clap his hands from behind the sofa, which really made Krupa jump from sofa and run into the kitchen, which was hilarious. Later everyone became serious and was engrossed in the movie while Ankit had his hand moving around Ira's waist and snuggling and lightly kissing her exposed neck and shoulders. As soon as that happened, without realising it, she leaned on him and was letting him have her. While when, she glared her eyes at Krupa she was already sitting on Sid's lap and not looking at the movie while Sid was caressing her and watching the movie intently.

Before the movie could have an end Ankit got up and said/announced, we are sleepy and pulled Ira to the room. Krupa chuckled and said, "Ankit, wear your pilot's cap and fly high together." Ira just smiled at the memory of Ankit who had licked his fingers and his flirtatious eyes. Back in his room, he sat on his bed and made Ira sit in his lap. Looking at him, he had his hand in her hair and pulled her in for a kiss. He pulled her close, so close that they could feel the warmth of their breath and the smell of the liquor. They sat in the same position for a few minutes until Ankit got his Pilot cap and placed it on her head, smiling, he leaned in for the kiss. It wasn't one of the aggressive ones that she had experienced in the lift rather it was soft and full of feeling of being cared for, of being loved. She liked that but now it was she who was being greedy for him, the way he had licked his fingers had made her horny. She pulled his hair so hard that it broke the sweet kiss and he was staring and asking if something was wrong and saying sorry with his eyes. But he didn't know what she had in her mind. She pulled him back again and gave a hard kiss on his lips. It was her tongue that was doing the dance and that drove Ankit crazy and aroused him too. He pulled her dress up and was happy to see her breasts and started handling them not with care, licking and sucking them. He played with them while she was enjoying it, she pulled his shirt off him and started kissing his neck while tingling him on his nape. She kissed him from his face to his shoulders, soft kisses and a few wet kisses that made him moan. She caressed his back and pulled him into her for more. He got the que and he ripped off his pants off and made her lie down and him on top. He kissed each and every exposed part of hers. His eyes were darkened with lust that was visible even in the dark while she had a smile that asked him for more, more and some more. He parted her legs and wanked her off the pretty panties that she was wearing and grinned, saying "Nice colour, and I smelled them." This made her crazy and she couldn't think any more. She was just so drunk and happy that nothing else mattered. He stooped low and started licking her and fingering her which drove her wild. She had never experienced this and started to moan in enjoyment, but then she kept her own hand on her mouth as she knew Krupa was outside and she was shy. He pulled out his weapon and rubbed it against her vagina while she begged to fuck her. He slowly inserted it inside her and started out slow as he knew it was her 1st time; slowly and steadily he started and then he couldn't control himself and increased the speed. Ira was moaning, and was lively. She guided his hand to her vagina and he knew what needed to be done, and that really made Ira see the gates of heaven and have her 1st ever orgasm. He wanted to change position so he pulled her up and, on her knees, she went and he was behind; she just knew that she was enjoying it and didn't want to stop and that is what he got her. They tried different sex positions and each one made her feel loved at its peak. After a while, when both were tired Ankit collapsed on her and said, "I hope you're satisfied, I hope you enjoyed, because I did." This made her smile and he could feel that smile even in the dark. Later they cuddled up in each other's arms naked and when he realised that she was getting cold, he got up and got a blanket and tugged her and himself in. He was sleeping on her shoulders and his hand on her breast, which he would squeeze every time he moved while she had one of her hands on his while the other in his hair, they slept together for an hour or two.

Ira was jolted awake by her phone ringing. She picked it up to see that it was Juhi calling again. Answering quietly, she said, "Good morning, Juhi." Juhi's voice was filled with concern as she demanded, "Where are you two? Are you okay?" Ira reassured her, "Yes, we're fine. Don't worry, we'll be back in an hour or two," before ending the call.

As Ira glanced at the clock, she saw it was nearly 8 a.m. Ankit, who had been watching her, urged, "Just a little more sleep." Ira explained that she needed to leave because Juhi was worried. Ankit chuckled and replied, "Why does she act like your mom? You're not doing anything wrong, yet."

Before Ira could get out of bed, Ankit drew her close for a kiss and said, "I'm not ready to let you go just yet. How about we have another round?

Morning Sex! as he exclaimed, and before she could say anything, Ankit had already started fingering her and asking for permission. She gave it and said "OKAY! Just one position then I will go." He then slid himself onto her while she was lying on her back, with each of his thrusts, she would push herself in as well and that drove him to moan her name out loud. It was like both of them were thrusting each other to be on the peak. A slight knock-on door made him jump out of bed and he said, "We are almost there Krupa stop knocking and leave us alone." That made Ira giggle a bit, and she scolded him and said, "I am coming Krupa, just give me 2 min."

Ankit had a sad face that said, "Please don't go," but when he saw Ira looking for her dress, he got up and helped her dress by zipping it up. She turned around, kissed his forehead and said, "This was the best 1st sex ever, so thank you for that." And as she was approaching the door, she turned around and chuckled, "Well I don't have anyone else to compare to so, it is going to be best, right?" With a wink.

That drove him to jump on her and push her to the door. He pulled her hands to the back and kissed her hard and held her as well. When she couldn't bear him doing that, she pushed him away and opened the door. Outside, Krupa was looking both ready and sleepy. She said, "We should head back before Juhi shows up here and drags us out herself."

Ankit and Sid came over to the lift to say their goodbyes, promising they'd see each other again. While the cab waited downstairs, Ira and Krupa stepped into the lift. Ira glanced back to see Ankit with his fingers in his mouth. With a playful smile, she called out, "Don't lick your fingers, Ankit!"

Both Ira and Ankit burst into laughter, sharing a light-hearted moment as the lift doors closed. In the cab, Krupa rested her head on Ira's shoulder and said, "I hope you had an amazing time. I can see that smile isn't going anywhere." Ira grinned and replied, "He definitely wore his pilot's cap before taking off!" Both of them erupted into laughter, their joy filling the cab.

Krupa then added, "Juhi will want all the details, so you'd better be ready." As Krupa fell asleep during the ride, Ira reflected on the experience. It truly was the best she had ever had—her first intimate encounter with someone as captivating as a pilot, like something straight out of the books she'd read in college. The image of Ankit licking his fingers kept making her blush.

It was an experience beyond words, matching everything her friends had told her about. Being held and loved by someone she barely knew had made her feel truly desired again. She knew her fiancé wanted her to have these experiences, but she wasn't sure how or if she would share the details of her adventure with him.

The reunion planned, with friends of old,
And memories shared of tales retold.
The things they'd said, the dreams she'd spun,
Imagined moments, held by none.

Time and again, her friends would say,
"Love and hugs will smooth the way."
A touch to ease the pain that drained,
A comfort soft, like hope regained.

She dreamed of warmth, the life to live,
And waited long for love to give.
The wait was worth it, for in time,
She found a spark, a rhythm, a rhyme.

The captain of her life took flight,
No metaphor for joy that night.
He started swift, then changed the pace,
Slow and sure, with gentle grace.

Like droplets of a quiet rain,
Their laughter washed away the pain.
Through whispered tales and smiles unseen,
They wove a night both soft and keen.

Today, that night is fresh and clear,
A memory held so close, so dear.
When days are hard, it lights her way,
And brings a smile to chase the gray.

She closes her eyes—she feels it now,
The joy that lifts her from each frown.
A gentle warmth, like sunlight's gleam,
Reviving moments from a cherished dream.

The Two Woes

On the 2nd of July 2024, Ira woke up later than usual. She had stayed up the previous night watching a lacklustre movie, causing her to miss her morning spinning class. Typically, her day began with checking WhatsApp messages, but today was different.

Instead of opening WhatsApp, Ira opened a matrimony app. She had received a new invitation and decided to go through a few profiles. One profile caught her attention – Vinit Nayak. He was well-educated, holding a B.Tech and an MBA from California. He was based in Kolhapur, involved in his family's hospitality business, specifically a hotel called Vrushali, and was also running his startup, Kaizen Foundry, which specialized in aluminium castings.

Still lying in bed, Ira thought Vinit seemed like a good match. She messaged him, sharing her WhatsApp number and expressing her interest in meeting him. Satisfied with her decision, she closed her phone and pulled the blanket over her head.

Soon after, her phone rang, catching her by surprise. Annoyed at being disturbed so early, she reluctantly answered. To her astonishment, it was Vinit Nayak. They chatted briefly, and Ira suggested meeting on Saturday as she had plans with friends for bowling in Koregaon Park (KP) that evening. Coincidentally, Vinit was also staying in KP.

But instead of meeting on Friday, they decided to meet on Thursday itself which was the 4th of July. Vinit had called her, and they had decided to meet in Baner only as he was adamant on driving near her place. She thought this is the 1st time that someone had said that to her, and so she agreed after denying it multiple times, they decided to meet at 6pm. So, Ira got ready and was thankful that her father was out of town which would mean that she could stay out of the house till late and she hardly cared what her mother said to her as she a had very complicated relationship with her mother.

Anyway, Ira was ready to meet Vinit at 6 PM, but there was no sign of him – no call, no message. Concerned, she called him at 5:30 PM to check if he was going to be late. Casually, Vinit replied that he might be delayed as he was out with his sister and her friend at a temple. Upset, Ira, who valued punctuality, suggested cancelling their meeting and rescheduling. Vinit, however, proposed that she come to Koregaon Park instead.

Ira laughed at his suggestion, firmly reminding him that they had agreed to meet at a midpoint. She was unwilling to travel to KP at 6 PM, knowing it would take her at least two hours to get there. Reluctant to waste her evening if Vinit turned out to be different from his online persona, she stood her ground. Eventually, they compromised on meeting in Kothrud, a midpoint between the temple and her location, though it was 7 km for him and nearly double that for her.

They both arrived at Pimlico Café simultaneously. There was Vinit, dressed in black and fluorescent shorts, a bodycon T-shirt, and sporting afro hair. He had a dark complexion and carried a bag on his shoulder. Normally, Ira might have been critical of his appearance, but this time, it felt different. She greeted him warmly, and they both settled into the café.

Vinit appreciated the small café's pink and blue interior, with seating arrangements nestled in beds of pink and white roses, making it an Instagram-worthy spot. He ordered a guava mojito, while Ira, a coffee enthusiast, opted for a cold coffee. They exchanged brief stories about their families, lifestyles, and travel aspirations while enjoying their drinks.

When Vinit received a work call, Ira glanced at her watch and noted it was nearly 8:30 PM. She sighed with relief, knowing she still had time before her mother would call her at 10:30 PM. After his call, Vinit suggested they go to Koregaon Park, offering to drive and drop her back later.

Ira hesitated, calculating the logistics. Travelling to KP at that hour meant reaching there by 9:30 PM. Spending at least an hour there, followed by the return trip, would have her home by 2 AM, which was unacceptable to her. Reading her hesitation, Vinit assured her that he would drive her back, even if they only spent an hour in KP. Reluctantly, Ira agreed, deciding not to spoil the mood for either of them.

They reached KP in about an hour in his car which was a Skoda some sedan model, and he parked his car in his sister's apartment. Then Vinit asked her, "Hey Ira, care for a walk if you are not that tired?" Ira loved to walk, she had stated before, and thankfully she was not wearing heels and she was up and said, “Yes,” with a big smile on her face.

Koregaon Park, popularly known as KP is Koregaon Park is a prestigious and vibrant neighbourhood in Pune, known for its lush greenery, upscale residences, and cultural significance. It features the Osho International Meditation Resort, attracting global visitors seeking tranquillity. The area is a culinary hub with diverse restaurants and cafes, and offers lively nightlife with popular bars and clubs. It boasts boutique shopping, and green spaces for outdoor activities. This blend of luxury, culture, and convenience makes Koregaon Park one of Pune's most desirable localities. This blend of luxury, culture, and convenience makes Koregaon Park one of Pune's most desirable localities. There are several lanes in KP which included the houses of reputed millionaires in Pune and also boast an array of cafes, restaurants, and eateries, catering to diverse culinary tastes. From local Indian delicacies to international cuisines, food enthusiasts will find plenty of options. Popular spots like German Bakery and Dario's are favourites among locals and tourists alike.

They began walking through the lanes, sharing their life stories, including their college dating experiences and other personal anecdotes. Vinit openly talked about dating his ex-wife, detailing how they met and fell in love, as if they were long-time friends catching up. The conversation flowed smoothly, touching upon their bodily needs, how they managed their anxieties, and past experiences.

As they strolled, Vinit pointed out notable landmarks, including the house of Poonawalla, the owner of the Serum Institute, and residences of other prominent figures like politician Sushil Kumar Shinde. He also showed her the house of Abhay Agarwal, a businessman notorious for the wrong reasons. Vinit recounted the infamous incident involving Abhay's son, Vedant Agarwal, who had killed two people in a car accident while driving drunk. The case was widely known, as the judge had sentenced Vedant to write an essay titled, "Why should a drunk person not drive a car?" This story had become a sensational piece of news in Maharashtra.

As they continued their walk, they exchanged more personal stories, deepening their understanding of each other. Vinit's willingness to share intimate details about his past relationships and personal life created a sense of camaraderie between them. Ira felt a mix of curiosity and empathy as she listened to his experiences and reflected on her own.

The evening air was filled with the scent of blooming flowers and the distant hum of city life. Despite her initial reservations, Ira found herself enjoying Vinit's company and the casual, honest conversation they were having. It was a refreshing change from the typical, guarded interactions she was used to in her quest for a suitable match.

After the long walk, Vinit suggested that they should have dinner, as it was a bit late, and they visited multiple restaurants but all were full and had a waiting for half an hour or more. Even on weekdays, its full; that was KP. Anyway, so Vinit decided to get a beer and sit in car, and drink and then have a small wrap or burger while driving back; she said to her, while Ira agreed with a smile. Before her mom could call her, Ira did call her younger brother Ishan and told him that she would be late and to handle mom and, he kinda did what she hoped, as she didn't get a call from her mother. They took 2 beers and sat in the car with AC on full speed and drank beer while vibing to the song. Vinit asked her if she was okay as she was sweating like hell, to that Ira replied, "Yes, I am good.

It's just that I am not dressed for a walk, I dressed up for a date and this top of mine is too thick for me to get any air inside." To that, Vinit was struck and they both started laughing. After a beer that she couldn't finish, Vinit remembered that she had told him that she wanted to pee, so instead of saying that there is no place, he took her home to his sister's place and apologised that no one really does, she said to herself. After that, Vinit took her to a small Seoul Bunsik, the Korean Café as she loved Korean cuisine. It was pretty late in the night and it was drizzling too and she wasn't feeling that hungry as well, so they ended up sharing one bowl of Chicken Toppokki. Later when Vinit saw Ira sneezing as it was too hot and spicy for her taste, he insisted on getting an ice cream, as he knew that she had a big sweet tooth, as was mentioned in the matrimony application. Ira said instead if he could drop her home and he agreed to drop her back to Kothrud. Back in the car, while listening to music, he held her hand and was humming to the music not saying a thing but just enjoying the company. When they reached back near her car in Kothrud instead of just saying good bye, he got out of his car and hugged her and said, Lets meetup tomorrow for breakfast at the Vohuman café and then spend the day together." She was bit sceptical but agreed on it.

After the long walk, Vinit suggested they have dinner since it was getting late. They visited multiple restaurants, but all were full, with waiting times of half an hour or more. This was typical for Koregaon Park (KP), even on weekdays. Undeterred, Vinit suggested they get some beer and sit in the car to drink, then grab a small wrap or burger while driving back. Ira agreed with a smile.

Before her mother could call, Ira contacted her younger brother Ishan, asking him to handle their mom. She hoped he managed well, as she didn't receive any calls from her mother. They bought two beers and sat in the car with the AC on full blast, vibing to the music while they drank. Vinit noticed Ira sweating and asked if she was okay. She admitted she was fine, but her thick top wasn't ideal for a walk, and they both laughed.

After struggling to finish her beer, Ira remembered she needed to use the bathroom. Instead of dismissing her, Vinit took her to his sister's place, apologizing for the unconventional stop. Appreciating his thoughtfulness, Ira decided to let it slide. Afterward, Vinit suggested they visit a small Korean café called Seoul Bunsik, knowing Ira loved Korean cuisine. It was late and drizzling, and Ira wasn't very hungry, so they shared a bowl of Chicken Toppokki.

As they ate, Ira started sneezing from the spiciness. Noticing her discomfort, Vinit suggested getting ice cream, aware of her sweet tooth from her matrimony profile. However, Ira asked if he could drop her in Kothrud where she had parked her car instead. Vinit agreed and drove her back to Kothrud.

During the drive, they listened to music, and Vinit held her hand, humming along without saying a word, simply enjoying her company. When they reached her car in Kothrud, Vinit got out and hugged her, suggesting they meet for breakfast at Vohuman Café the next day and spend the day together. Sceptical but intrigued, Ira agreed.

He hugged her and bid her goodbye. Ira drove home, listening to classic Kishore Kumar songs, a big smile on her face. It had turned out to be a good day. She arrived home around 2 AM, just as she had calculated, and was pleased to find her mother asleep. As she changed her clothes, she replayed the day's events in her mind, feeling like everything had fallen perfectly into place.

The next morning, Ira tried on various outfits, wanting to choose the perfect one for her breakfast date with Vinit. Eventually, she settled on a simple shirt and jeans, deciding that he should see her dressed casually and confident. She then started driving towards Vohuman Café.

Vohuman Café, located on Dhole Patil Road, was founded in 1978 and is one of Pune's most iconic Irani cafes. Renowned for its delicious and affordable breakfast options, especially the cheese omelette, bun maska (buttered buns), and Irani chai (tea), the café retains a nostalgic atmosphere with simple wooden furniture, vintage posters, and friendly, unpretentious service. It's considered a cultural landmark in Pune, representing the city's rich history of Irani cafés and the community they foster.

Ira arrived at the café earlier than expected, likely because it was Saturday and there wasn't much traffic. She walked around while speaking to Vinit on the phone, who insisted she keep talking to him as he was running late and didn't want her to get bored. After about ten minutes, she saw him sitting in his car, unable to find parking nearby. Vinit asked Ira to join him in his car so they could find a parking spot together and then walk to the café.

After parking, they walked to the café, and Vinit ordered a cheese omelette with double eggs for himself and a regular masala omelette for Ira, along with two buttered toasts and two Irani chais(tea). Ira, not a fan of cheese overpowering the eggs, reluctantly accepted his choice. They ate while sipping the famous Irani chai.

Vinit began talking about his ex-wife, Niharika, recounting how they met at a rave party in Goa, became friends, and started dating. He shared details about Niharika being a dermatologist and how she visited him in California during his MBA, supposedly for a conference that got cancelled, leading her to stay with him. They spent several weeks together, growing closer. As Vinit continued, Ira found herself lost in thought. She appreciated his openness but wasn't sure she was ready to hear so much about his past. She thought to herself, "It's his trauma to deal with, why is he telling me all this? I hope he doesn't start talking about their sex life."

Vinit went on about Niharika's obsession with having a child and how she manipulated him into marriage for that purpose. He admitted he was in love and attached to her, which led to their marriage. Unable to listen any longer, Ira cleared her throat and suggested they pay the bill and leave, as people were waiting for their seats. They settled the bill and walked towards the car.

Before Vinit could resume his story, Ira asked, "So, how do you want to spend the day?" Vinit smiled and asked, "Can we smoke weed together?" Taken aback, Ira responded aloud, "Weed, really?" With a grin, Vinit nodded. Despite her surprise, she agreed, thinking that even if he wasn't the right guy, at least the weed might be amazing. She saw it as a test he wanted her to pass to secure a place in his mind.

They bought rolling papers and a few juices; in case they got too high and needed to sober up with pomegranate juice. Though unsure how the juice would help, Ira didn't question it. When she asked where they would smoke, Vinit suggested his Airbnb apartment. Ira hesitated, worried about the implications of getting high and potentially doing something she would regret, especially if he had any bad intentions. Her guards were always up, and she knew what was right and what wasn't.

Sensing her concern, Vinit reassured her that nothing would happen and that it was entirely up to her whether she wanted to smoke. He left the decision open, showing respect for her boundaries. This is what she liked about him as he understood that she had her guards up and that she was smart enough to know things even before anything even happened. They reached Vinit's Airbnb which was in Viman Nagar.

It was a cute little 1bhk apartment with a huge dog picture that was painted on the wall and both of them being dog lovers loved it. Then there was a small swing in the living room for kids to swing on and a sofa set, with a small dining table near the kitchen for 2 people. Then there was one bedroom with a wooden hedge over it and a long white curtain-like things that was draped on the wall with a small bit of lighting. The room was decorated with small plants here and there which were attached to the small balcony with a green fake garden and 2 high chairs to sit on with a view of the canal. It was quite a cozy apartment and the television was placed in the bedroom. Now, that was weird is what Ira thought, but he dismissed it to not think further about it.

They sat on the high chair in the balcony for some time to enjoy the view of the canal and the weather as it was still drizzling a bit. Ira closed her eyes to soak it all in and enjoy the moment. It was the 1st time that she was here with someone she hardly knew in this apartment not knowing what would happen. She was a bit excite, and a bit tense but still decided to let go off a bit and let it flow, the quote that she hated. She knew her boundaries that she had set for herself to save herself from implications later on. Looking at her, Vinit called her inside the room, and they started rolling the weed in the cigarette as Ira had earlier said 1 smoke would do no harm. They tried to put on some music but there was some problem with the television, so Ira got her laptop out and played some music. They did light the cigarette and smoked it up. All of a sudden, Vinit got up and started dancing to the song and pulled her in as well, she was overwhelmed, and she danced in as well, a bit of salsa and a bit of rowdy dance they did till the weed got over. Vinit suggested that they should watch a movie and stated that there is new movie on Netflix. While Ira thought they would see some Romcom movie to enjoy the mood, he selected the movie Maharaj.

The movie Maharaja stars Junaid Khan, son of Amir Khan, where he plays the role of Krasandas Mulji who was mid 19 – century journalist, author and social reformer in Bombay and Gujarat. The film is based on a real-life liberal case that happened in 1862. It is based on a novel called "Maharaj" by Saurabh Shah. It was about how women were treated poorly and how they had to sacrifice themselves to the Maharajas as a slaves just for a night. And how one Journalist took a stand for them and made people aware that it is wrong to do so. It was indeed a powerful movie.

1st movie date, both were maybe high and they decided to watch the most enticing movie Maharaj. Ira was taken aback when Vinit suggested this movie but didn't say anything and played the movie. There they sat on the bed together, hand in hand with each other and watched the movie in silence. He was engrossed in movie and maybe Ira was a bit high and looked at him staring at the laptop as she wanted more, like maybe a kiss or something as she looked at his lips. "Stop it, Ira!!!" She said to herself. Focus on movie or it will go wild. She took a deep breath and sobered herself with that juice that they had got and watched the movie. They spoke about how badly women were treated during that era and how badly they treat them now as well while the movie was still playing. They discussed their beliefs and boundaries that one should respect and follow as well as the god that they worshipped. After the movie was almost, over Vinit suggested ordering food as it was almost 3 pm, which was quite late as they had breakfast at 9am.

Vinit ordered lunch from Mr Merchant in Ira Nagar, another new restaurant that had just opened. The cuisine they had was Middle Eastern, Arabian, Lebanese and Mediterranean. They had quite a big spread of food and being foody he did ask if Ira eats lamb; to that, Ira smiled and said, "I eat everything that moves, except humans." To that, he laughed and said, "Same." He ordered mutton kebab, mutton mandi and lamb and mint. The food was delivered within half an hour and they enjoyed the yummy food while Vinit started his story which was left in morning, about his ex, Niharika. By this time, she was annoyed and said to him that she knows how wrong your ex-wife was but can we please stop talking about her and talk about us instead? To that, Vinit didn't say a thing for a while and then said that he wants to share all the things that had happened to him and also wants to hear what happened with her in detail.

Ira started telling her story, "My marriage to Kartik was arranged by my parents. I met Kartik just 3 times and then as a medical coder, my job required intense focus and adherence to strict protocols, which often meant leaving my phone outside the workspace. This added to the difficulty of maintaining a connection with Kartik, who lived and worked in London. We had met only a few times before our arranged marriage, and most of our communication was limited to phone calls, further hampered by the significant time difference. It felt like we were strangers bound by societal expectations rather than genuine affection. In May, we legally formalized our marriage to expedite my visa process, with the actual wedding ceremony scheduled for December 2019. After the wedding, we went on a short vacation to Goa, which was supposed to be a prelude to our life together. Instead, it turned into a revelation of our incompatibility. Kartik's dismissive attitude towards the trip, referring to it as "not the honeymoon" but just a small vacation, left me feeling uneasy and disillusioned.

Moving to London was supposed to be a new beginning, but it quickly turned into a nightmare. On our first night, Kartik asked me to sleep in the living room because I had a cold. He claimed he didn't want to get sick, as he had to work the next day. This pattern of avoidance continued, with Kartik frequently using various excuses to avoid sharing a room. Eventually, I moved my belongings to a separate room permanently. It was clear that physical and emotional intimacy was not something he valued.

The COVID-19 pandemic struck, making it impossible for me to find a job despite my qualifications and experience. Kartik's salary was reduced due to remote work, and instead of supporting me, he suggested I work as a cleaner to contribute financially. This suggestion was not only insensitive but deeply insulting, considering my educational background and professional achievements in the medical field. His lack of support and understanding left me feeling humiliated and undervalued.

The breaking point came when Kartik insisted, I ask my father for money. This led to a fierce argument where I reminded him of my father's financial contributions to our wedding and criticized his lavish spending habits. The emotional neglect reached its peak when I suffered a severe burn while cooking. Despite my pain, Kartik showed no concern for my wellbeing and continued indulging in his games and shows. His complete lack of empathy and care shattered any remaining hope I had for our relationship.

My marriage to Kartik is a testament to the importance of mutual respect, empathy, and understanding. Our relationship, marked by neglect and insensitivity, serves as a cautionary tale about the dangers of entering a marriage without a strong personal connection. Despite the numerous challenges, I have learned the importance of self-respect and assertiveness. My journey through this ordeal has strengthened my resolve to stand up for myself and seek the respect and empathy I deserve in a relationship." And that is about it; it was well defined and nothing that I would change if given a chance to relive it again.

After listening to my story, Vinit was incredulous. "It's impossible that you had no physical relationship with your husband," he said, shaking his head. Then he asked, "And then what happened?" I felt a wave of exhaustion and finality wash over me. "That's it," I replied, my voice firm. "I'm over it, and it was like it never existed. I'm sorry, but I don't want to get into the details, even if you want to share."

"But Ira," Vinit said earnestly, "I want to share. I want you to understand what I went through. I want to be an open book."

She glanced at her watch. "It's 5 pm," She said, standing up. "I better start from here if I want to reach home by 7 pm. I'm sorry, but I need to leave. It's getting late, and yes, as you said, we have indeed spent the entire day together." Vinit nodded, understanding her need to leave, and booked a cab.

As Ira packed my things, Vinit suddenly reached out and held my hand. "Let's get married," he said, his eyes intense.

She stared at him, shocked. "Already? You want to get married after just two days? Wow, that's fast, don't you think?"

He looked at her with determination. "Take my dad's number and tell your dad to call him. Let's get hitched."

She was taken aback by his sudden proposal, but I nodded. "Okay, I will talk to my dad." They hugged each other tightly, neither of us wanting to let go.

Soon, the cab arrived. I got in, bid him goodbye, and watched him as the car pulled away, my mind a whirlwind of emotions and possibilities. While travelling back home in the cab, she realised how smoothly all things had happened. All the things that really bothered her in a guy were mere nothing when it came to Vinit. It felt as if it was what it was meant to be. Is he the one that she had got from God for the 16 Monday fasting that she had done (sola somvar is the fast that is done for 16 Mondays to get a good husband as per Hindu mythology, it is said that when Parvati did this sola somvar vrat, she got a husband as Shankar Bhagwan/ god) or is it that she was being too positive about things she thought to herself? But that didn't stop her from writing down a few words, The day we met was all so new,

I came forward, knowing nothing of you.
The first time we met, it felt so right,
A missing piece is now in my sight.

Time alone, just me and you
A puzzle solved a love so true.
Your hand in mine, it felt so dear,
As if it always belonged here.

The first hug, the dance we shared,
A warmth so deep, a bond so rare.
You listened so close, you wanted to know,
A conviction so pure, a love to grow

In your pain, I see your plea,
For a hug to calm, you like the sea.
Serenity and peace, I hope you find,
In the love and comfort intertwined.

Above and beyond, we have both strived,
To be together, to be alive.
Our longing deep, our love so clear,
Together forever, the love that we will preserve.

The next morning, Ira sat down with her dad to tell him about Vinit. "Dad," she began, "I met someone on the matrimony site, and we've agreed that it's time for our parents to meet." Her dad listened attentively as she showed him Vinit's profile. After reviewing it, he agreed that Vinit seemed like a good match. He promptly called Vinit's father, and they arranged to meet on Sunday at 4 pm at their house in Baner. Both Vinit and she were over the moon. They spent hours talking on the phone or on video call, never far from each other's thoughts, no matter the time of day.

They were already dreaming about their wedding and the sangeet. Vinit mentioned that he wanted to get six-pack abs for the occasion, while she laughed and said, "I might shed a few kilos but love my curves just the way they were."

However, their conversations sometimes veered into darker territories. Vinit often spoke about his ex-wife and the tumultuous relationship they had. He recounted how she didn't want to have a baby, how she got pregnant and had an abortion without telling him. These stories made her pause and reflect, but she let him talk, thinking it was better for him to get it all out now, so our future together wouldn't be haunted by his past.

Vinit told her about Niharika's behaviour—how she would leave early in the morning, claiming she had appointments, only to go back to her parents' house for breakfast. Deep down, she sensed that Vinit might still be entangled in the emotional drama of his past. Despite this, she stayed positive and believed that, in time, he would move on. He also shared that their divorce had been smooth because her parents acknowledged there was no way out, given their daughter's mental health issues and her need for medication. As she listened to his stories, she was struck by the pain and complexity of his past. Yet, she hoped that by airing these grievances now, we could start our life together on a clean slate, focusing on the future they wanted to build.

A week had flown by, and Sunday had finally arrived. Ira's father had invited her elder sister, Meera, and her family over, making it feel like a family reunion. By 4 pm, Vinit and his parents arrived, and the introductions began. It was a typical "pohe program," where the guy and his family come to meet the girl and learn more about her life and family.

Ira's father and Vinit's father chatted about work and family, while Vinit's mother kept a watchful eye on Ira. Sensing this, Meera jumped in to extol her sister's virtues. She highlighted how Ira was the tallest and most attractive among the siblings, her love for cooking and reading, and her dedication to continuous learning and professional growth.

Then Vinit's mother spoke, suggesting that Ira and Vinit should spend more time together before making any decisions. She then compared Ira to Vinit's ex-wife, which felt like a cruel blow. Meera immediately defended her sister, stating that comparing Ira to Vinit's ex-wife was not only unfair but also damaging. She emphasized that Vinit and Ira were adults capable of making their own decisions and that knowing someone deeply could take years. Meera argued that trust and gut feeling were crucial and insisted that Vinit should give Ira a clean slate.

Vinit's mother was taken aback by Meera's words, and his father then turned to Ira, asking, "Beta, can you tell us why you divorced your ex-husband?" Before Ira could answer, Vinit stood up and interjected, "I know why she got divorced, and I've already told you about it, Baba. Come on, Ira, let's go out for a drive." The room fell silent, everyone staring at them in surprised. Meera encouraged them to go, saying they needed to spend more time together.

As they got into the car, Ira turned to Vinit and said, "You should have let me answer your dad." He replied, "There's no need. I don't understand why he's trying to make you feel low, and I don't like that." Ira smiled, appreciating his protectiveness, and said, "Thank you, but I could have handled it." Vinit took her hand and reassured her, "Don't worry," as he drove off.

When they returned, everything seemed to have been discussed, and everyone was waiting for them. Within ten minutes, Vinit and his family were ready to leave. Ira's father said he would call with a decision, and as they were saying their goodbyes, Vinit winked at Ira, whispering, "All done and ready to get married now."

Back home, a serious discussion unfolded at the dining table. Ira's father began, "Ira, do you know that Vinit is not divorced yet? His mother kept saying that they haven't got the papers yet and it will be November when they shall get the papers." This revelation stunned Ira, leaving her momentarily speechless. Her sister, Meera, spoke next. "Ira, his mom kept comparing you to his ex-wife and mentioned that you need to fast for four days a week and shouldn't go out of the house often. Did you know that?"

Then her brother chimed in, "I think they are frauds. They kept talking about his ex, and maybe they are still involved with her. Maybe you should stay away from them." Her father spoke again, more measured this time. "Ira, listen beta, if he can show you the decree of divorce and if you think he is the right person, I will do a background check for him. Then we will see how things go after that."

The barrage of opinions and questions hit Ira like a bolt of lightning. "What? He is not divorced? But he told me his divorce was smooth! What the hell?" She thought, feeling a whirlwind of emotions. "Fast for four days? When will I be allowed to eat? And his mom comparing me to his ex—that's just too much." Overwhelmed, she simply said, "Okay, I will see," and left the table.

Later, her brother knocked on her door and suggested, "Ira, let's go out for dinner, just you, me, Meera, and Anya." Ira agreed, needing a break from the intense discussion. At the restaurant, Mekong Folks in Balewadi, they were joined by Rhea, their niece.

As they settled in, Ira made an announcement. "I don't want to talk about Vinit today. Give me some time to think, and then we can discuss it." Everyone agreed and shifted the conversation to lighter topics. They ordered drinks, and Ira chose a Citrus Martini without checking the ingredients. After one sip, her head started spinning. She checked the ingredients and realized it contained 60ml of gin and 150ml of orange juice. The combination, coupled with her empty stomach and the day's stress, made everything around her spin. She found it amusing and laughed as her vision blurred.

They enjoyed a variety of dishes, from sushi and inari to kebabs and bao for starters, and rice with lamb curry for the main course. Dessert was also on the menu. Despite the tumultuous day, the dinner provided a much-needed distraction and comfort. The atmosphere at Mekong Folks was inviting, and the food delicious, offering a brief respite from her troubles.

As soon as Ira got home, she changed her clothes and jumped onto her bed. She had a bad headache and was a bit tipsy; all she needed was sleep. Before going to dinner, she had informed Vinit that she was going out with her siblings, but she hadn't called or texted him any more than that. She didn't know what to say. The next day, when Vinit called, she didn't answer. Instead, she sent a brief text wishing him a happy journey and mentioning that she needed time to think. Vinit didn't push for a conversation, which gave Ira the space she needed.

To clear her head, Ira decided to go for a drive, an activity that always calmed her down. She needed time to think about what to say to Vinit and how to approach the situation. Despite her efforts, she couldn't come up with a solution on her own, so she decided to meet her best friend, Jyoti, who might be able to provide some clarity and support.

Ira called Jyoti and suggested they meet at Yaki, a restaurant on Deccan known for its Asian, Thai, and Japanese cuisine. In the past, they would go to a good pub, enjoy drinks, listen to music, and talk, but now their meetings were centred around good food and meaningful conversations. When they met, Ira shared the whole incident with Jyoti, who listened attentively.

Jyoti, sensing that something was amiss, told Ira that she had suspected something was wrong. She offered her views and advice on how to deal with the situation. Feeling somewhat relieved after the conversation and the meal, Ira thought she might have found a way forward.

A couple of days later, Ira called Vinit. "Vinit, I'm sorry that I have been MIA since our family meet, but the way your mom said that you are not yet divorced really shook me to the core. It made me realize that the moments we had and the dreams we saw together are all shattered. I didn't know what to say to you or if anything I said would even matter."

Vinit sighed deeply. "Ira, I told you about the papers that I will be getting in November, and I did say that I have an affidavit allowing me to get married. Moreover, you asked for my father's number and said, "Let's get married as soon as possible."

This threw Ira off her composure. Furious, she said, "I'm sorry, what did you say? When did you mention that you don't have a decree of divorce? I never asked you or anyone else for their dad's number. What are you talking about? With all the crap you've told me about your ex-wife, you failed to mention that you don't have a decree of divorce. I never asked for your father's number. You were the one who said, "Let's get married and willingly give me your father's contact details, telling me my father should call yours. You are such a liar, and thank God I know this before anything further could happen. Thank you, but no thank you. I am not interested in you or your stories about your ex-wife."

With that, Ira hung up, feeling a sense of relief and closure. She realized that she had narrowly avoided a complicated and potentially damaging relationship, reaffirming her belief in her own strength and judgment. This was the second time someone had humiliated Ira in front of her parents since her divorce. The first time was with a guy named Punit Pavaskar, whom she had met through the same matrimony app. Punit was an engineer who worked in his family business, owning a jewellery shop and a restaurant. What drew her to him was his decision to work with his family and stay in Sangli, a choice that resonated with her values. She met him multiple times and had known him since May 2021, even before her divorce was finalized.

Punit seemed like the perfect fit. He was planning to expand his restaurant business to Pune, knew his goals, and accepted Ira as she was, despite having had compatibility issues with his ex-wife. They often met and talked, and Ira even said she wouldn't mind staying in Sangli to bake and make a living. Punit would laugh and say, "Sure, why not? I can help you with your business as well."

She had discussed Punit with her father, who was okay with the match because Punit was well-educated and seemed to know what was right and what wasn't. Once, Punit called Ira and said he would come and meet her parents in the evening around 4 PM after he finished his work. Ira was delighted because they had already discussed the kind of life they wanted to build together. They had given several months to a year or more for their love and respect to blossom. They discussed boundaries, growing old together, how many kids to have, and how to raise them in the current generation. They had discussed it all. Punit's father even called Ira's father to say they would come and meet soon.

That very day, Ira met Punit for breakfast and discussed how tense he was about meeting her father in the evening. But when evening came, there was no sign of Punit. It was as if he had vanished into thin air. Ira called him repeatedly, but there was no response. She realized it was all a lie. A few days later, Punit called her and said, "My father said don't meet her parents alone. We should all meet together." But that was it. No further contact ensued, and all of Ira's dreams were dashed.

These experiences left Ira feeling disillusioned and hurt. It seemed like every time she tried to move forward and build a new life, the past came back to haunt her, making it difficult to trust again. Despite the setbacks, Ira knew she had to keep moving forward, but the scars of these experiences would take time to heal.

I made me lonely,
I made me care,

Once again, I'm the one
who thought all is fair.
I put my guards down,
now they need to rise,

Higher than ever,
touching the skies.
Trust is what I need
to slow it down,

Love will never bloom,
lost in the town.

Far gone in the cocoon
again,
Wrapped tightly,
escaping the pain.

No one can seep in,
not even slightly,
A ray of sun, distant,
barely lightly.

I've bound myself once again,
you see,
Guarded and hidden,
forever to be.

A moment of Realization

After countless ups and downs, Ira knew she had suffered greatly. She tried to be the good girl her parents always wanted, but nothing she did aligned with their expectations. She believed herself to be a daughter any parents would love, even if she wasn't the top student, but a last bencher. Yet, she never stopped studying, always upgrading herself to keep pace with others.

Her father, a diabetic, was ruthless with his diet, leading to high blood sugar and frequent illness. Ira accompanied him to every doctor and appointment. With her medical background, she understood his reports and often advised him to stay away from Google searches.

Ira vividly recalls when her father once insisted, he had a brain tumour after months of severe headaches, following his own online research. She took him to every appointment, from the family doctor to the neurologist, ensuring he got all necessary tests, including an MRI. Despite initially trying to explain that his symptoms didn't indicate a tumour, she resorted to reverse psychology, letting him undergo all tests so the doctors could assure him he was fine. Her laughter was uncontrollable when he booked an appointment with a neurosurgeon, convinced the tumour needed removal. In the end, the tests confirmed what she had said all along: there was no tumour.

Her attentiveness contrasted starkly with their so-called son, who dismissed their father's pain, suggesting Ira let a driver take him to appointments. This neglect spoke volumes about him, their parents, and their upbringing.

Ira loved people and cherished friends, even if her family didn't provide the support she needed. She chose her friends carefully and made them her family, finding love and companionship in them.

Once, Ira and her sister Meera went out for coffee, and it was there that Ira received a shocking revelation. Meera, with a serious tone, said, "Ira, I need to speak to you. Listen carefully. You are being emotionally abused by our parents, and maybe you can't recognize it because you were abused by your ex-husband too. The feeling you had living with him for that one year is so ingrained that now, when anyone abuses you, you can't recognize it. You think you'll be loved if you do as they say."

Ira looked at her, confused and thinking, "Emotionally abused? What is she talking about?" So she asked, "Meera, can you elaborate? I'm not really getting it when you say emotionally abused and by parents."

Meera continued, "Listen to me. You do everything as Father says, and when you deny, he makes you feel guilty, and then you just give in. The same with Mom. When she says, 'Ira, you need to cook and learn to make things,' I know you can do all that. You don't need to do it now. You are well-trained, and Ishan and his wife Anya should take responsibility for our parents, not you. Otherwise, you'll become like Ujwala Atya."

They fell silent for a while. Ira thought about Ujwala Atya and realized, "Hmmm, that makes sense." Ujwala Atya was her dad's younger sister who agreed to everything her mother and brother said. Now, she was admitted to an asylum for being mentally unstable. Despite her extensive education, she lost her sanity after her mother passed away, and now she was uncontrollable, forcing their father to admit her.

This realization hit Ira hard. It dawned on her that she had been following a similar path, unknowingly succumbing to emotional manipulation, and it was time to break free from this cycle for her own well-being. Meera continued, "You need to stop working like a slave in that house. You need to get a job and leave permanently. They need to realize you have a life too. Remember how you complained about them being on your back, asking a million questions about your whereabouts, and not allowing you to stay out late? What's the worst that can happen if you come home late? They'll bad-mouth you and be disappointed? So what? They never take your side anyway, so why should you keep suffering no matter how good you are to them?"

Ira, lost in thought, began to understand what her sister was saying. She knew she needed to break free. She looked at Meera and said, "Meera, I really do hate you sometimes, but thank you for telling me this. You've made me realize I need to live for myself and be a bit selfish to maintain my sanity. So thank you. I will be mindful about the things I do and don't."

Meera added, "It's okay if you don't find someone to marry. Just have a boyfriend in the meantime. Or forget about a husband altogether—you can have a great life without one. You can build a life for yourself and enjoy it instead of being stuck in one place or with the wrong person."

Ira smiled, "Yes! That's what I've been saying all along, while everyone was pressuring me to find a good husband, as if that's the only way to live." They both smiled at each other, sharing a moment of understanding and newfound freedom. Then later in the evening, Ira thought about what she had discussed with her sister and made a few rules for herself, more like guidelines so that she would know if something was wrong. To actually allow herself to see with open eyes and follow it with conviction as a part of self-preservation.

1. Maturity is finally to stop trying to convince people to treat you right, you observe what they are doing and if you don't like what you're observing.
2. You communicate that something is bothering you.
3. And after communicating, your feelings aren't validated, and you are not respected, then you just walk away.

Maturity is not about chasing, nor is it about begging; it's not about giving everything all your energy to someone who continues to disrespect you. Maturity is putting my well-being first. Now Ira had chosen to see the truth and she knew that if they cared, then it would reflect on their behaviour and now, she knows how people actually think of her. Her own family treated her as an object and made her feel low when she was at her lowest. There was no regard for how she feels or what she was going through. Ira had always been a person who thought that people are good and you should see good in one as it is easy to see bad things, but saying that things will get better got her nowhere. Nor with her parents, nor with her ex-husband and so it was time to let go of what she thinks is right and watch what reality is. It was easy; she always thought that things would change and her parents would understand her one day, but that one day didn't come in the last 35 years, and now it's time to give up for her own happiness that she needs to seek.

Ira recalls a scene from the movie "Cha Cha Real Smooth" where the actor asks, "Have you been depressed?" The actress responds, "I have always been depressed." The actor then inquires, "What is it like being depressed?" She replies, "It feels like you don't know what better feels like, and you do things that you think will make you feel better, but they don't. In fact, they make you feel worse. The things I'm really scared of doing are probably the ones that would help me the most, but I just can't do them." At that moment, Ira realized they were both in the same boat.

And that is what she did, and she started following the guidelines which actually had started showing results. It did make her feel guilty but then she had to do it; she knew that now, and now no one can take advantage of her being good, is what she thought every time when she felt guilty. She had learned to live for herself, embracing her own strength and worth.

Ira then started giving up tasks that drained her, like going to the vegetable market with her mom on Sundays. Her mom insisted she needed to learn it, but Ira finally said, "Mummy, I can get vegetables on my own and I can cook them too. I don't think I need to come with you every time. I won't be joining you anymore." Her mom was shocked and started complaining.

Whenever her dad asked about her whereabouts, Ira simply replied, "I went out, and that's the only answer you're going to get, so please don't ask questions I might not be able to answer." In the evenings, when she met friends for dinners, she would answer her mom's call at 10:30 PM and say she'd be late, urging her mom to go to sleep.

When Ira came home late, her mom would criticize her, but she decided not to feel guilty for her own happiness. Once, she got angry at her mom for not having lunch for her. Her mom dismissively said the food was gone, and Ira could make something for herself. Her dad sided with her mom, saying it was important for Ishan to have food since he had come home for lunch.

That day, Ira was frustrated that she even had to fight for basic food. She didn't speak to her mom at all. When her dad tried to smooth things over, she bluntly told him, "You can't decide when I get to be mad and when I need to let things go." Her dad, taken aback, said nothing, knowing her mom was at fault.

Ira's journey as a consultant for international students at a local institution has been both rewarding and challenging, offering her a taste of real-world workplace dynamics, friendship, and the push for professional growth. She has a passion for her role, even though it involves long hours and a gruelling commute which she undertakes daily with an unwavering smile. Her primary responsibilities include drafting and reviewing SOPs (statements of purpose) for students applying to universities abroad. However, her enthusiasm is dampened by her senior colleague Sakina, who consistently works to sideline her by restricting her attendance at meetings and minimizing her interactions with students, as if Ira's success might pose a threat. Despite these hurdles, Ira maintains a calm resolve, finding solace in the knowledge that this job, although demanding, was never meant to be a long-term career path. Still, the strain of dealing with Sakina's behaviour is visible enough that even other colleagues recognize her frustration.

At the beginning, other employees had cautioned Ira about Sakina's difficult personality, but Ira was unfazed, assured in her work ethic and confidence that she could handle any situation. She had expected some office politics and was prepared to endure a heavy workload or even subtle mockery, but Sakina's determination to isolate her was an unexpected level of hostility. Despite these challenges, Ira found support and friendship among her colleagues, particularly with Disha and Lalita, who became her close friends. These small bonds brought her a sense of relief during breaks from the daily grind. Disha's routine of tapping on the partition glass for a quick chat, and their shared humour over preferences like whiskey or beer, became highlights of Ira's day. Lalita, who was married and experienced in the ways of navigating relationships, was a patient listener when Ira needed to vent, building a sense of mutual understanding and trust that helped Ira break down some of her own guardedness.

In a workplace composed entirely of women, Ira initially felt out of place, but over time, she found herself enjoying the camaraderie and humour among her colleagues. Gossiping about each other's lives and exchanging light-hearted complaints became a part of their daily routine. Her friends and co-workers like Shreya, Aliza, Jahnvi, Shraddha, Sayali, Ameesha, and Messiah each added their own stories and perspectives to the workplace, adding a new dimension to her daily interactions. Ira's habit of arriving early to avoid the anxiety of being late also led to a unique bond with Messiah, who often joined her for coffee and the latest updates on office gossip, reinforcing Ira's sense of connection within the team.

The turning point came with an upcoming education fair, where each consultant was assigned a university to represent alongside an international delegate. Sakina, who was vocal about her preference for representing a German university, was disappointed to learn that Ira, instead, would be handling ISM (International School of Management), while Sakina was assigned to a university in Ireland. Sakina's frustration was visible to everyone, as she tried to get the assignment changed, but was unsuccessful. Ira, initially unaffected by Sakina's complaints, recognized this as an opportunity to prove herself and secretly began preparing to handle all aspects of ISM's offerings and requirements. She meticulously studied the university's admission process, scholarship details, and even local regulations about student work hours in Germany. She even took the extra step of subtly asking Sakina a few questions to gain more insight, under the guise of curiosity, further strengthening her knowledge base for the fair.

When the day of the fair arrived, Ira was poised and well-prepared, a fact that was evident when her international delegate unexpectedly cancelled. Undeterred, she took charge of her assigned desk, confidently counselling parents and students on the admission process, part-time work regulations, and the support they could expect while studying abroad. Her first interaction with a parent was smooth and satisfying, boosting her confidence and easing any remaining doubts about her abilities. Even her boss, Renu, was reassured when Ira confidently conveyed her readiness, noting that her practical experience studying abroad had uniquely equipped her to counsel students on their journey. With this newfound confidence, Ira embraced the fair as a chance to showcase her knowledge, proving to herself—and to her sceptical senior—that she was more than capable of handling the role independently.

By the end of the day, Ira had counselled nearly 35 students and parents, impressing her colleagues as they passed by her booth, complimenting her on her confidence and the ease with which she handled everyone's questions. Even Renu mam, her boss, stopped by to check on things and was pleasantly surprised to see Ira handling it all independently. Ira had proven herself ready to take on the role of an independent counsellor. Once the fair wrapped up, her colleagues eagerly dashed to the washroom to freshen up for their planned dinner, but Ira, exhausted, remained seated, just wanting a moment of peace. Her jaw ached from all the talking and explaining. She had picked out a casual, flowy blue short dress for the evening, knowing that after such a long day, she'd likely be worn out. Her friends, however, were buzzing with energy, eager to kick off the night. They all got ready, snapping hundreds of photos before piling into Ira's car and heading to Publiq for dinner.

Being a Saturday night, Ira expected the restaurant to get busy with people, laughter, and music filling the air. She nursed a recent leg injury, so dancing wasn't in the cards for her, but she relaxed with her drink, taking it all in while her friends kept up with their pictures and excited chatter. Many of them were thrilled to be at a pub-style venue for the first time, posting their night out on Instagram to commemorate the occasion. Ira, familiar with places like these, chose to sit back, savour her drink, and enjoy the moment. Once the photoshoot was over, they regrouped at the table, ordering a few pasta dishes and pizzas, glancing cautiously at the prices. Ira decided to treat them to nachos, which brightened their mood even more. Money wasn't an issue for her, but seeing their happiness was a rare treat she valued.

When the food arrived, conversation flowed, and everyone shared a bit about themselves. Ira opened up, talking about her past experiences, including her divorce and job journey, satisfying some of her friends' curiosity about her. The others shared their own stories, with Lalita warmly talking about her husband. The evening was both relaxing and invigorating, a perfect close to a hectic day. Ira was starting to really enjoy these outings with her work friends, even as she noticed that those not invited to dinner showed a bit of envy the next day, peppering them with questions about where they went and when they returned. Ira understood these social dynamics well, having seen them before.

As Navratri approached, another plan took shape: an evening of dandiya at Mahalaxmi Lawns. Ira was excited, recalling that it had been ages since she last danced dandiya. Initially, she thought about renting the full traditional attire, with a "Ghagra Choli," a bright dupatta, large earrings, a necklace, maang tikka, and bangles. But short on time, she decided to wear the sangeet outfit she'd bought for her brother's wedding—a chic, deep-neck blouse paired with a black skirt decorated with pink, mirror-like straps, and a cape. She finished off the look with simple earrings.

The evening turned magical, with Ira dancing energetically despite the pouring rain. She even joined in on Garba, dancing away her worries. Though she wasn't feeling her best, she found herself lost in the music and rhythm, enjoying every moment. Ira had learned the art of enjoying even when she is down or not feeling like as she believed that you need to take chances on being happy as life doesn't leave you with having a bad/sad moment.

But, as always, there was a catch. Despite the thrill of proving herself at the fair, working with Sakina was becoming increasingly unbearable. Sakina didn't even bother asking Ira about her experience or congratulating her. Instead, the first thing she said when Ira returned was, "I hope you didn't counsel anyone or give out wrong information. I'm sure Renu mam realized that and pulled you from the booth."

The frustration of being treated like a nobody, like someone just there to serve, finally got to Ira. For the first time, she responded directly to Sakina. "Oh no, Sakina mam," she said, keeping her voice calm yet firm. "I actually enjoyed it a lot. I was the only one counselling students and parents, and, you know, I do have hands-on experience with studying abroad. Being a former student, myself helped me provide guidance better than anyone else. In fact, Renu mam told me I'm an asset to this company after seeing me in action!" Ira smiled tightly, adding, "All thanks to you, Sakina mam. Watching you counsel all those times made it a piece of cake for me."

She watched Sakina's face fall, her surprise barely hidden, before Sakina turned and left the cabin in a rush, heading straight for Janhvi and Disha. Ira couldn't help the quiet laugh that escaped her. Looking through the glass wall, she saw Disha giving her an impressed look, shaking her head as if to say, *"Wow, Ira, just wow." * Ira shot her a sheepish smile in return, complete with a mischievous glint in her eye.

Ira knew she had stirred up trouble with her playful jab at Sakina, and it wasn't long before the repercussions began. Sakina wasted no time, filing complaints that Ira spent too much time on breaks, claiming she wasn't taking her work seriously. She even went as far as saying Ira was wasting time around the office instead of working. When Ira confided in Disha and Lalita, they laughed, noting that Ira was practically glued to her laptop all day, and they had to drag her out for breaks. Disha even suggested that Ira should bring it up with their branch manager, but Ira knew this would only fuel an unnecessary conflict she wasn't prepared to escalate. She had taken this job for a low-stress work environment, and reporting Sakina would ruin that. Instead, she bit her tongue, followed instructions, and meticulously documented all her work at the end of each day, ensuring there was no way for Sakina to misrepresent her efforts.

However, over time, the tension took its toll. The stress was building, and Ira realized that standing up for herself was necessary—she couldn't endure the emotional strain any longer. She deserved respect and a healthy work environment, and she was done sacrificing her peace. Rather than reporting Sakina, Ira submitted her resignation to Minoti, the branch manager. When asked about her reason for leaving, Ira laid out the details: she explained how poorly Sakina had treated her and provided a record of her workload as proof of her commitment.

Minoti promptly called Renu, their boss, into the conversation. Renu and Minoti both expressed regret that Ira hadn't formally complained about Sakina earlier, assuring her that they would have addressed the issue. But Ira knew this would only have led to an uncomfortable cold war, something she'd never signed up for. Instead, Renu shifted the conversation, explaining that Sakina was one of the company's top performers, consistently bringing in more students and profits. She advised Ira to take note of Sakina's effectiveness and learn from her.

Calmly but firmly, Ira replied, stating that while Sakina might be successful with students, how she treated her colleagues mattered too. It wasn't just her who had issues with Sakina; others struggled with her, but either couldn't or wouldn't speak up because they didn't work with her directly. "I'm sorry," Ira said, "but there's a reason so many people who worked closely with her have left. I won't stay here and subject myself to that." She finished with a polite but resolute, "I'll be submitting my official resignation by email. Thank you."

As she walked out of the office, she felt a deep sense of relief wash over her. "Peace is what I am looking for, and nothing else matters," she whispered to herself, finally feeling free.

Gone are the days, and gone are the winds,
When I believed we were one, on the same page.
You instilled guilt in me, making me feel it deep,
I was just a toy, wound tightly by your hand.
The more you turned the key, the more I danced,
At every moment, whenever you got a chance.

You used me, pursued me, as if I were not your own,
Filling me with despair, you left me alone.
The walls closed in, hitting me with culpability,
You turned a blind eye, shirking your duty.
You made me yearn for love and empathy,
I met people whose eyes reflected sympathy.

Desperately, I'd say, "I like you now,"
No matter how flawed they might be,
And saw myself bow.
They walked over me, round and round,
Leaving me back at zero, crumbling me down.

You shattered me to pieces, now and always,
You stayed the same, despite my endless praise.
But now I reclaim my life, I own it fully,
No matter what you do, I'll stand strong and truly.

Bias Parenting - Mental health impact on Daughters

Growing up, Ira often felt like a guest in my own family. From my earliest memories, the rules for Ira and her older sister, Meera, were different from those for my brother. It was as though our entire existence was a training ground for silence, obedience, and sacrifice, while Ishan was free to be loud, demanding, and even hurtful. What baffled me the most was the way her parents would brush off his behaviour with excuses, while every step Meera and she took was measured, criticized, and often ignored. This double standard ran so deep that even my emotions and opinions felt like they didn't belong to me; they were things I was expected to suppress for the "greater good" of the family.

I noticed early on that, boys held a special status in our family. I remember how my mother would tell us stories of other families who had sons, how they were "lucky," and how parents blessed with boys were respected in society. Having a brother only made this comparison worse. I watched him receive praise for even the smallest achievement, while Meera and I were reminded of our "duty" to be humble, supportive, and patient. It wasn't jealousy I felt, but frustration, a deep aching disappointment that no matter what I did, I would always be a step behind, simply because I wasn't a son.

The emotional scars ran deeper as I grew older. Whenever I tried to voice my feelings, my parents would dismiss me as being "too sensitive" or "too rebellious." Once, I overheard my father laughing with his friends, making light of Meera's husband's career. I saw her hold back tears, and when she later tried to confront him, he simply shrugged it off as a joke. That was our reality—our pain was trivialized, our self-respect was optional, and any attempt to assert ourselves was met with ridicule or silence. Watching Meera suffer like that left me angry and helpless. It was clear that my feelings would be treated no differently; my family's habit of minimizing our feelings was something they didn't even see as wrong.

On one hand, he supported Ishan financially both during his studies and after he joined the family business, while Meera and Ira were left to earn their own living fighting alone with office politics, bullying, low pay and tedious travel arrangements. But as they were built as strong and independent people, they were up for any struggles in life; they knew what respect was and now they can fight for the same outside their house. Both Ira and Meera were different people outside the house, they were well mannered, educated, respected and they liked that as back home they were nothing to their parents or to their brother. Ira still remembers her father's story that he proudly tells at least twice a month as being a proud father. Stories of how Meera struggled in the early stages of her marriage when they were living in Germany and how they barely had money to survive which in turn led to eating food just once a day and how her father once gave Meera 100 euros. He tells it proudly, describing how Meera had come to see him off at the train station, looking sad, and how that small amount brought a big smile on her face.

On the other hand, now that Ishan is making a substantial income in the family business – despite doing relatively little work, he still receives a large sum for his expenses along with a large amount as his salary. While Ira earns less than 5% of her brother's monthly income. For her father or for Ishan 100 euros is just like a tip, something they might casually leave at restaurant. Yet they feel that they have done plenty for her, yet the bias that Ira and her sister have to endure is the unbearable pain.

Imagine the situation reversed – if Ishan was in Germany earning a modest income, their father would likely be sending him as much financial support as possible. It's no wonder Meera and Ira see their father's jokes as hurtful, while he just dismisses their feelings as if they were trivial.

In our house, respect was never earned; it was demanded. Ira's parents held this unshakeable belief that their children owed them respect simply because they were our parents. Yet, they never once considered how their words or actions affected the girls. They were reminded constantly that they should be "grateful" for everything they did for them, even if it meant tolerating their scolding, their dismissive jokes, and their public humiliations. They acted as though we, especially Meera and I, had no right to ask for understanding or kindness in return. While their brother, however, was never required to demonstrate this same respect. In fact, his small accomplishments were treated like grand achievements, while their successes were just expected and taken for granted.

For years, Ira tried to accept this imbalance, to ignore her own anger and hurt. But each time when she saw Meera get scolded for the smallest things or be made to feel guilty for simply speaking up, Ira felt the weight of her own silence grow heavier. It's painful when the people who are supposed to love you unconditionally only seem to see you as a shadow, an accessory to their own lives. There were days she would wonder if she would ever be able to stand up to them, to make them see her as more than just a daughter who could be moulded, criticized, and silenced. The thought of finally speaking my mind was terrifying but also filled her with a strange sense of relief.

There was one point where Ira tried to explain her frustration to her parents. Ira took all the courage that she had to tell them that she deserved respect too, that she wasn't asking to be placed above anyone but just to be treated as an equal. But before Ira could even finish, they dismissed her. "What do you know?" they scoffed. "We've given you everything you could ever need, and this is the thanks we get?" Their reaction was crushing. Instead of hearing her out, they turned her plea for respect into an accusation, painting as the ungrateful daughter who dared question her family's love. Ira soon realised that her father was showing the narcissistic behaviour as in whenever, she tried to put her thoughts or asked questions, her father would turn against her and make her believe that she is at the fault, that made her angry- real angry.

Her brother, meanwhile, remained untouched by these expectations. He could do as he pleased, insult their parents or ignore them, yet his behaviour was met with excuses and second chances. His failures were passed off as "youthful mistakes," while Meera and I were expected to hold up the family's honour, regardless of our own dreams or desires. Even on the worst days, when he showed complete disregard for them, he was still the favoured one. It became clearer to Ira that no amount of sacrifice or obedience on her part would ever earn the same acceptance.

As I, Ira, stand on the threshold of adulthood, I am torn between love for my family and the painful truth of their unfairness. It's difficult to reconcile the fact that the people who raised me, who should have been my biggest supporters, are the same people who have caused me so much heartache. I want to hold onto the hope that one day, they will see me not as a responsibility but as a person, deserving of the same respect and freedom that my brother so effortlessly receives. I don't know if that day will come, but until it does, I'm learning to find strength within myself. Because, in the end, respect isn't something I should have to earn—it's something we all deserve, simply because we are human.

Once when Ira was really angry with her parents, she went to her sister's place just said nothing and played with her niece. When Meera observed her closely, she made a cup of coffee for her to spill the beans. Later the Ira told her that she has made a plan on how she is going to treat her parents the same way their son treats them so they would understand or start respecting their daughters as well. After listening to that Meera laughed a bit and said, "Ira we both are sensitive people and we can't hurt our parents; no matter how much we try to, that guilt would kill us and we won't let that happen." There was silence for a moment, Ira said again, correct I can never behave like him ever in my life and then she kept on staring at Meera and said, "Meera, you are going to be an amazing mother; the one that we never had, your daughter is lucky to have a mother like you."

Taking back my life - By Enrique Iglesias

Ira is currently in an "I hate men" phase, which she finds herself unable to escape. Despite this, she is content, and her happiness is what matters most. She now resides in a spacious bungalow in Baner with her brother Ishan and his wife Anya, while their parents have moved back to their old apartment in Kothrud

The decision for the parents to move back was driven by their inability to adjust to the traffic and hustle of Baner, as well as their disapproval of their children's lifestyle choices. The sarcastic remarks from both mom and dad drove everyone in the house crazy, often leading to back-and-forth arguments. Understanding that constant arguments were not beneficial, the parents chose to relocate to a place that was more physically and mentally comfortable for them.

Ira's parents tried to persuade her to move with them to Kothrud, using emotional blackmail. However, Ira, having turned her life around, was determined to stay in Baner. She made it clear that her life was now rooted there, with her gym, friends, and job occupying her six days a week, leaving one day for rest. Ira was well aware that moving to Kothrud would mean taking on the household responsibilities, managing appointments, and dealing with her parents' incessant nagging about marriage and her reliability. She knew this would only add unnecessary stress to her life.

Ira acknowledges that her parents have not neglected her. They provided her with everything they thought she needed, from education to jewellery for marriage, a car, and even a house. However, they failed to give her what she truly wanted—understanding and respect for her individuality. They saw material support as a solution, but Ira wanted her identity and choices to be respected.

The lack of empathy and respect from her parents took a toll on Ira. Despite being grateful for their sacrifices, she felt that her efforts and sacrifices were not acknowledged. When her parents began to bad-mouth her without any fault of hers, Ira decided it was time to distance herself.

Ira often finds herself creating stories about meeting someone through a dating app or a matrimony site, just to keep her parents at bay. Yet, no matter how hard she tries, they fail to see how their behaviour suffocates her. For them, Ira is not a person but a problem to solve—a burden they're desperate to offload.

Once, her father coldly remarked, "Even your younger brother thinks you should leave the house. He's not wrong. You better find someone, or you'll end up alone."

Those words cut deep. They weren't just hurtful; they reignited the eating disorder Ira had fought so hard to overcome. Food became her solace, her reflex—a desperate attempt to fill the void their rejection left behind. It showed on her; her appearance fluctuated in every photo, her body reflecting the weight of her emotions, both joy and sorrow. Yet no one seemed to notice—or care.

Her younger brother stayed silent through it all. He understood that voicing agreement with their father's harsh words would only deepen the divide between him and his sisters. He respected Ira's strength, quietly acknowledging the fire she carried within her.

His wife, however, was different. Sweet and gentle, she saw beyond Ira's defences. While she might agree with her husband in private, her kindness toward Ira was unwavering. She often said, "Ira, you need someone to talk to when you come home. You're not going anywhere."

Those words warmed Ira's heart in a way few things could. They brought a genuine smile to her face—a rare, fleeting moment of relief amidst the chaos.

Ira is now happy living in Baner, having carved out a life for herself. While the issues with her parents remain unresolved, she is content with her decision to prioritized her happiness and live life on her terms.

Given all that, Ira has transitioned to working as a baker professionally, who has clients in the form of small cafes where she sells her famous chocolate chip cookies and also makes delicious biryanis as per order. She is part-time writer who pens down poetry and is well satisfied in work that she loves to do. Ira aspires to become an entrepreneur just like her elder sister, she plans to open a small café with healthy food be it low-carb food and desserts that she loves to make. She is also planning to be an inhouse Biryani chef that people can hire her to make some lip-smacking biryani for them. She is busy with work and laughter she shares with her life as of now.

Every other Saturday, Ira meets her friend Jyoti for a drink or two, where they share gossip and life stories. Sundays are her days to unwind; she either lies in bed all day or cooks and bakes, dancing to music with her sister-in-law.

Life is good now. She spends her weekdays watching crazy movies in the evenings, enjoying drinks—whether it's beer or coffee—with love and laughter in Baner. It has been a couple of months since her parents moved to their new apartment, and Ira isn't looking forward to seeing them. She is healing and enjoying her life. Although she often receives calls from her father, she engages in a pleasant chat but maintains her boundaries firmly.

Ira is still active on matrimony and dating apps. She selects her own dates, presenting a different personality and story to each one but never oversharing. She prefers to meet people on weekday evenings so that a bad date doesn't ruin her day. Late-night talks with her girlfriends and staying out late help her live in the moment.

Many things have changed in Ira's life, but she still enjoys going out for coffee alone to savour the silence, watching movies alone, and eating a huge bucket of popcorn. She is still looking for a partner but is no longer desperate. She is willing to wait for the right one. She is also okay with the idea of living alone, as she now knows that she is happy and content in her life, and nothing can ruin it.

Her parents, of course, are still on her case and occasionally try to blackmail her emotionally. However, her ever after is the peace she has found in love, laughter, and the people around her. The books she reads continue to inspire her.

The life she sought, the path she chose,
A journey carved by none but her own prose.
With strength unyielding, fierce and true,
No one could sway her, no winds blew through.

A Taurus soul, her spirit unmoved,
Like stone she stands, her will proved.
She may not know each thing she seeks,
But clear are the bounds she'll never breach.

In romantic novels, she finds delight,
Silent movies watched through endless nights.
She believes in a love that will remain,
Unbound by time, untouched by pain.

Alone she walks, yet free from strife,
Unfazed by couples and their woven lives.
For in her heart, she's found her peace,
A quiet strength, her sweet release.

She plays with dreams, with lovers unseen,
Imagining hands that hold her keen,
A love that lifts her, hand in hand,
To chase her dreams across the land,
A distant hope, a dream yet afar,
Guiding her heart like a steadfast star.